The Youngster

BIBI BERKI

Deixis Press

Copyright © Bibi Berki 2025
All rights reserved.

The right of Bibi Berki to be identified as the author of this work has been asserted by her in accordance with the Copyright, Designs and Patents Act 1988.

This book is a work of fiction. Names, characters, businesses, and incidents either are products of the author's imagination or are used in a fictitious manner. Any resemblance to actual persons, living or dead, events, or locales is entirely coincidental.

First published in 2025 by Deixis Press
www.deixis.press

ISBN 978-1-917090-08-7 (HB)
ISBN 978-1-917090-09-4 (PB)

Typeset using Bulmer MT by
Palimpsest Book Production Ltd, Falkirk, Stirlingshire

Cover design by Deividas Jablonskis

The Youngster

BIBI BERKI

Prologue

In the car that morning Beatrice had said, entirely casually, innocently, like a child speculating about space flight: "I wonder what it feels like to kill someone. Not the guilt afterwards, not remorse or anything like that. But actually perpetrating the death of someone with your own hands. *With your own hands.* Knowing exactly what you're doing as you're doing it. What must that feel like?"

There had been a silence, then, between them, not out of shock or the inability to follow up those spoken thoughts, but because they required further contemplation.

Georgie, who was driving, had shuddered and looked for an excuse to stop the car. Said she was momentarily disorientated and had pulled over to the kerb.

"Oh, I'm so sorry!" Beatrice exclaimed. "I shouldn't have said that."

"It's fine," Georgie soothed the younger woman as she yanked up the handbrake. "Absolutely fine."

But the truth was that she, too, had found herself considering the very same question of late, had heard it being asked somewhere just beneath her consciousness. What *would* that feel like? To deliberately, knowingly, end a human life? To watch your hands in the act, to hear the final breath, to see the light go out and to know that you had put it out. Would it be instantly transformative? Would you cross over to another you as soon as it had happened? Would you have to *be* another you to do it in the first place and look on like a spectator while the act was carried out? Would it be awful? Would it be physically demanding? Would it be – for that moment – fascinating?

Would it be a relief?

As they sat there, Georgie had found herself back in familiar territory – trying to cover up her anxiety, putting a calm face on a moment of panic. She had taken out her phone and looked blindly at it, pretending she was getting her bearings. But she felt the familiar pain in her chest arriving and her breathing was hurrying, falling over itself, and she didn't want Beatrice to notice that anything might be physically wrong with her. So, she waited, pretended she was trying to remember the route, all the while calming herself and her breathing so that things could appear as normal.

The two women had looked ahead through the rain-washed windscreen, neither daring to glance at the other, both still asking themselves how they could even be uttering such vile thoughts and knowing that the mere act of speculation meant that they had indeed probably crossed to some other place. A place where most people would never go in their lives.

PART ONE

1

From a distance, they could have been the same age. Two older women, sitting on a park bench on an overcast late winter morning. One slight and neat, her legs – in tights and long, heeled boots – crossed at the ankles, and her gloved hands on her knees. The other larger and looser, her overcoat open to reveal jeans and trainers, and her position constantly shifting, her arms and legs never at rest. The smaller one had a trim little knitted hat over her beige-grey bob. The uncovered hair of the other one was long, dark and with curls that were sometimes not curls but simply mess.

It's only if you walked a little closer, passed directly in front of that bench, that you'd see you were wrong. They weren't the same age at all. The smaller one was older than the larger, her face pretty but her soft, dim eyes disappearing beneath her mascara and eyeliner. The larger one had no make-up on at all and her face was agile and taut, the lines coming from frowns and general consternation.

And soon, although they looked nothing like each other, from their starkly different body frames to their dress sense, you'd realise they were mother and daughter. Maybe because of the way the larger one grabbed the hand of the smaller one every now and again and placed it on her lap, like she was looking after a wayward pet. Or the way the smaller one smiled proprietorially at her companion, nodding indulgently, listening, captivated. Or maybe it wasn't anything that either said or did or suggested. Maybe it was simply the very evident love that passed back and forth between the two of them and enclosed them in their own little world with a population of two.

*

"Well," said the mother. "They don't pull their punches, do they?"

The daughter frowned.

"Don't read too much into it. They always exaggerate, doctors. They do it to cover their backs. The fear of litigation. The fear of arsey patients. Just plain fear."

The mother was thinking about it, left her hand in her daughter's lap.

"When it happens. When I can't think for myself, I might just…"

"Might just what?"

"Let myself disappear. Remove myself."

The daughter wanted it to be clear that she was outraged.

"No, no, no, no. We're not having this conversation. No way. It won't happen."

The mother said nothing for a moment. It was impossible to argue with her daughter, even when it was about her own life.

"And besides," said the daughter. "I'm here. I'm always here. Nothing will change that. We'll do what Dr Croft suggested. We'll talk. Always. About the past and about plans for the future. We'll keep that beautiful brain of yours going and going. It won't have a chance to…"

"To disintegrate?"

In the park, despite the cold, the people seemed energetic and brisk. A family made up of two parents, three young children and a dog, passed by the bench like a circus caravan. The mother and daughter smiled and nodded at the parents. On the other side of the green, an elderly couple was heading towards the lake path. They stopped to wave.

"Who are they?" asked the daughter irritably.

"Nice people. They live in one of the alms houses, lucky buggers. I'm sure I mentioned them before. He used to own the carpet shop. You remember?"

"No."

"She's lamb-like. Very sweet kind of person. Two sons, I think. She says he's had affairs all the way through the marriage but that she hasn't minded because she doesn't like having sex with him."

"Good grief. She told you that?"

"People," said the mother, "tell me all kinds of things."

"It's because you'll stop to listen. I wish you wouldn't."

The mother pursed her lips against a smile. She watched her daughter grab at her hair and twist it between her fists, as she'd done all her life. It broke the hair shafts, created frizz, but what could you say after all this time? You can't stop a person. It's her hair, after all. Her habit.

"Mama," said the daughter, heaving round to face her. "I've worked it all out. We carry on walking, just like we've done for the past few years. The same days. We just stick to our routine. That way you'll have something concrete in your day. We'll meet like we always do, on Thursdays, Fridays, Saturdays and Sundays at the top of your road. We'll do the same circuit – past the cemetery and into Priory Gardens – and then we'll have our tea at Frank's. Always. Nothing will stop us. And while we do it, we'll talk about the things we love talking about. About your garden. Your plans for the garden. Yes?"

The mother was nodding and smiling.

"Yes, darling. We'll do all that. But you've got a husband and a son and I haven't. They're your priority."

"No, they're not."

"Yes, they are."

The daughter wasn't having it. She had an urge to explain, to lay it all out. She needed to plan. You could tell. Planning meant succeeding.

"Yes, of course I've got them and they mean everything to me, but it's different to what *we* have. It's been you and me always. Well, nearly always. The odd ruction but otherwise."

"I've been thinking about that of late," said the mother. "I'm sorry that there were times when I wasn't all I should have been to you. That I was a bit, well, unorthodox as mothers go."

"Mum! You were perfect. *It* was perfect. But while we're at it, I'm sorry I was such a difficult and obnoxious little brat as a kid."

This was beginning to feel like a final reckoning and neither was comfortable with the thought. The mother led things back to the positive.

"Nonsense. You were adorable. It was good, though, wasn't it? The places we lived, the adventures we had. But it's funny how tiny things that seem so important and eternal just disappear. I remember that I always stacked the mugs in the evening one on top of the other so that you had yours to hand first thing in the morning when you made your tea before school. It was vital. Ceremonial. Is that the word?"

"I don't remember. Where was that – the Dulwich flat?"

"Yes. And now it's gone. Just gone. Doesn't mean a thing. Something so important then and not now. I shouldn't really remember it at all. Nothing stays, does it? Everything changes."

"I suppose so," agreed the daughter.

The mother reached for the daughter's hands, held them in her own.

"*We* won't be the same for ever. *This* won't. In fact, it might already be changing."

"No," said the daughter. "We'll keep it going. It's nowhere near over."

"I've been thinking," began the mother.

"Oh here we go."

"It was the mugs that did it. You see, everything that ever happens to a person simply leads to the now. The now is all that counts. And one day the now will be our death."

"For goodness' sake!"

"Don't you find that reassuring? *I* do. It's all so ephemeral. Like a party."

They sat in silence for a moment, watching a group of teenagers, all in black, shuffling and scrambling towards the old ornamental gardens, an air of desperate danger coming off them.

When the daughter spoke, she did it quietly, her eyes trained ahead, her thoughts arriving one at a time, new and unexpected.

"I need you, Mama. I need there to be two of us. Maybe it's because I grew up like that, with you and no one else. That's the arrangement I like. It's either me alone or one other person. A close person. I like the feeling of having someone there, next to me, someone I can turn to. A kind of other me. And I think you're the same."

The mother's voice, when it came, was loose, like her words were floating out of her.

"Yes. I know what you mean. The reaching out and knowing you'll definitely touch someone."

"Exactly."

If you were there, you'd feel it, too, it was so strong. The ancientness of them, experiences stretching back into days neither could even necessarily remember. Roots that had spread so far underground that they walked on them everywhere they went.

So much of what they had, had been forged in silence and over ordinary years. To speak like this was to admit to something. A premonition perhaps.

"I don't know why I feel so confessional today," said the daughter.

Her mother patted her hand.

"For the same reason I do. We've had a bit of a shock. But listen to me. Let me tell you how much you mean to me. Let me dispel any worries you might have about the past once and for all. No! Don't try and stop me. Who knows how much longer I'll make sense? If this thing really is going to descend on me as quickly as they say then I want to keep telling you how much I love you, how much I owe you, how much fun I've had since the minute you were born. These aren't just words. They're truths. Now is not the time for us to be stoical and stiff-upper-lipped. Now is the time to be honest."

When the daughter turned to her mother, her eyes were full.

"I'm not as good as you when it comes to things like this," she complained.

The mother was smiling, reached out to tuck the poor bruised hair out of the way of nervous hands.

"Yes, you are. You're going to have to cope in a way I couldn't. You're much more resilient than me. You've got the harder side of the bargain. I'll be in happy ignorance."

"Oh stop it."

"Come on. Let's accept. That's a start, isn't it? There's nothing we can do except relish every moment we have together. And you're absolutely right: let's keep talking…about the past and about the future. I'm terrible when I'm alone, just can't remember a thing. But when you're with me, everything is clear again. Let's do lots of exciting things. All the little things we both love so much. You were going to help me get those summer flowering bulbs in, remember?"

"Yes," said the daughter, pulling herself up, wiping away the dampness that had settled on one cheek. "Of course. And help you get a new compost bin."

"I've seen the one I like. I'm going to go ahead and order it. And then we'll…Oh, look."

A man was walking on the path opposite them, a good twenty feet away, his face turned towards them. The daughter could barely make out his features, his beanie hat pulled down so low that it rested on top of his glasses, and his cagoule zipped up tightly under his chin. He moved in a fussy, dainty kind of way, placing his feet carefully in between puddles.

"Who's that weirdo?" asked the daughter.

The weirdo waved by curling and uncurling his fingers and the mother waved back.

"Oh, just another of my many boyfriends."

"Mum! What is it with you and befriending people? You collect all the human detritus of this park."

"Well, I have to do something on the days you're working."

"But why such losers?"

"I don't collect them. They collect me. He's very bright, actually. Very interesting views on all kinds of things. But a bit of a lost soul. Darling, are you all right? Your voice sounds a bit craggy. Is that my fault? Have I got you all emotional?"

The daughter laughed, then put a hand to her chest and winced.

"I've got some bloody bug. Probably caught it at work."

"You don't think it's…?"

"What? No, no. It's a cold or a chest infection."

The mother's expression changed at once. She was suddenly in charge, alert, bustling.

"You're going home to sleep it off. You know what it's like with your asthma. It knocks you out."

The daughter, in reply, was just as abruptly docile and pliable.

"I do feel ludicrously tired. Every little thing seems a bit much." She could hear herself whining. "But what about tomorrow?"

"What about it?" said the mother, getting to her feet, gesturing for the daughter to rise, holding her arm in support.

"What if I can't come out? We're meant to go walking, sticking to our routine. It's essential. Dr Croft said we needed to stick to things. You might get forgetful again, might get confused. You need me here with you."

"Oh Georgie girl," said the mother gently, brimming with compassion for that curious, shambling bear of a beloved daughter. "A day or two apart won't kill us. What's important is that you get better."

She slipped her arm into the crook of her daughter's elbow as they moved off together. "And anyway, I've got any number of park boyfriends to keep me on the straight and narrow. Don't for a second worry about me."

2

Georgie stood at the foot of her stairs and looked up them. From where she was on the bottom step, the top one seemed so far away and so impossible to reach, that she sagged on the spot and started to cry.

"I can't," she moaned to herself. "I can't do it."

Her coat and gloves were on the floor where she'd dropped them. She had parted from her mother only ten minutes earlier. The idea had been to curl up in her bed and make herself well again with an hour's sleep. But how would she get to her bed?

She returned shakily to the sitting room and the sofa and took out her phone.

"Sam, I can't go up the stairs."

"Why not?" He was distracted, overloaded as ever.

"I just can't. You don't think I've got…"

"What? Oh that? No."

"Then what is it?"

"Gastric flu or something. You're dehydrated. Get yourself some water and go to bed and I'll sort you out when I get home."

"I haven't got anything for dinner."

She could hear her husband losing patience, that there were more pressing issues beyond the phone.

"I'm fine with cheese and crackers."

That's what he always said. They never had crackers in the house. And the cheese was just a block of cheddar for cooking.

"Gina."

"What?"

"Take a couple of Paracetamol and sleep it off. Don't worry about dinner. Bed. Now. You promise?"

"I promise," she said, but after ringing off, she simply tipped over on the sofa and almost instantly fell asleep.

*

In her dream, her mother had been walking ahead of her on their path, the one that ran alongside the cemetery. They reached its end and turned left, as ever, and walked along the grass verge only there was no park at the end of it. Instead, they came to a standstill, shoulder to shoulder, looking down into a quarry with crippled bikes and mangled pushchairs way beneath them. "People throw away perfectly good things," her mother complained. "Let's get them." "No!" Georgie had cried, but her mother simply launched herself off the edge and disappeared, leaving Georgie confused and crying.

When she woke up it occurred to her that she probably cried far too easily. She was crying now, feeling hot and uncomfortable, her stomach gurgling and her limbs coming loose. If someone were to place a glass of cold water into her hands now, she'd be beyond grateful.

She called her mother.

"Georgie girl!"

"You all right?"

"I'm very well indeed."

"I'm worried you've got what I've got."

"I feel as strong as a horse. But…"

Georgie listened to her mother's breath, the quiet hypnotic rhythm. Too much time was passing.

"Mum?"

"I'm just trying to remember."

Only the night before, Georgie had raised the issue with Sam than her mother was a different person when she was alone, when confronted with silence. In the park, she seemed her normal self. It was back in her house, isolated, that the damage always set in. Her mother was a talker and a responder. How could you respond to nothing?

Sam had listened but not contributed his own views and she was, as ever, left with her doubts and anxieties.

"I'm going to the kitchen, darling. That might help."

Georgie listened, heard the scraping back of a kitchen chair, her mother's fingers tapping on the tabletop, could picture the slight hand and the gold ring.

"Was it something we talked about today? The way we used to stack the mugs in the Dulwich flat? I love hearing your memories of those days."

"The mugs? What about the mugs?"

The fingers were still tapping. The breaths were speeding.

"Who called who, darling?"

"I called you, Mum. It's about tomorrow. If I carry on like this, I definitely won't be able to come out. I'm so sorry."

"Of course you can't, my love. What day is tomorrow, anyway?"

"It's Friday."

"I have something that I do on Fridays. What is it? I should have written it down. That's what they tell me to do."

How could this have happened? It had only been two hours since they'd discussed it. This is what Sam needed to understand. That Georgie couldn't leave her mother to fend for herself.

"You go for a walk with me. But you won't tomorrow. OK?"

"You're ill!" exclaimed her mother at once and in triumph. "That's it. I wasn't looking for something after all. Silly cow."

"But will you be all right?"

"Of course I will. I shall wave to the Youngster and he'll wave back. That's enough excitement for one day."

"Oh that's what you call him, is it?"

"Everyone gets a name. We're only at the waving stage, though."

Georgie laughed. "A nice slow courtship. That's what I like to hear."

She was aware that she was shivering and didn't want her mother to catch it in her voice. Somehow, she must drag herself to her bed and stay there for as long as it took. Suddenly, she longed for her husband to be at home, fussing around her and bringing her orange squash, which he always did when she had a cold.

"A bit of a lost soul," said her mother.

"Who?"

"The Youngster. You can tell he relishes company, even half-witted company like mine. He's had a difficult upbringing, I think. Did I say how polite he was?"

Georgie's mind was swimming now.

"You did."

"Sorry."

"I feel pretty terrible. I'm going to ring off. Sorry, Mum. Love you, love you."

"Oh bye darling. Back, back."

Georgie placed her head on to the arm of the sofa, just to rest for a moment while she made a plan for getting upstairs, and woke again an hour later soaked in her own perspiration.

*

She was in her bed at last. How she got there, she couldn't recall, but Sam was downstairs, clattering in the kitchen, the radio on. The news, of course.

From her bed she could look out onto the garden. It was dark outside but even during the day the garden was dormant at the moment, with Spring at least a month away. While Benjamin was young, the space had been not much more than a football pitch and a playground, with a sand pit and slide at the far end. But as her boy's outdoor interests waned, so Georgie felt she owed it to the house to improve the grounds. She had enlisted a reluctant Sam to help her re-dig the borders and cut back the overgrown shrubs. When it came to planting, she studied books and websites and bulk-bought bulbs and perennials and laid out a rather traditional design that she believed would be "easy-care". There was an Italianate terrace by the French windows where she placed antique planters with scented geraniums and beyond that was a kidney-shaped lawn surrounded by beds. Nothing imaginative or challenging. Just a scene that changed with the seasons and provided an engaging view from their bed. Thereafter, she employed a gardener to handle the drudgery of keeping it engaging and in the summer helped him by dead-heading and weeding. After a while, the view was dominated by swathes of self-seeded foxgloves and hollyhocks which needed next to no looking after, except pulling out by the roots once the summer was over. What a contrast to her mother's tiny outside space which was crammed with ferns and palms, a controlled mini-jungle, all green, very modern, next to no colour, and with a little table and chair where she could sip her coffee in the morning.

Sam placed a glass of orange squash on the bedside table.

"I'll have to call work and tell them I'm not well," she said.

He sat on the edge of the bed and felt her forehead.

"I'll do that. You just sleep it all off. Don't worry about anything. I'll sleep in Benjamin's room tonight so I won't disturb you."

He leant in but Georgie gestured him away.

"I don't want you catching this."

As he left, he turned at the door.

"I just don't know where you'd have caught it from. It can't be that. The numbers are so low and we haven't been abroad or anything." He was on the point of exasperation and Georgie was distantly surprised to realise that for once she didn't care or feel the need to soothe. She turned in her bed, faced away from the garden, and closed her eyes. Just one day of rest and then she'd be better.

*

The phone cut through her sleep. She found it difficult to lift her arm to the bedside table.

"Georgie." Her mother had been crying.

"What is it, Mum?"

"I can't remember if I sent it to you."

"What, Mum? What?"

"I saw a lovely dress pattern, just right for your shape, and I sent off for it and I don't remember what happened next. It was perfect for your bust size. Did you get it? Oh will it always be like this? The grey bits?"

Georgie tried to sit up but found she couldn't. The effort to speak and to do it reassuringly was more draining even than having to sit up.

"Everything will be all right, I promise. God, I hope you haven't caught my thing."

"Are you ill? I can't remember." Her mother's voice was trembling.

Georgie's arms, so frustratingly weak, already felt like they were circling her mother's shoulders. Tears – of course – were lining themselves up. They said it would be like this, that the slightest change of routine or the merest whiff of anxiety might cloud her mother's memory, throw her into confusion. It would pass but in the meantime she would seem distressed.

"Mum."

"What is it?"

"I'm finding it a bit tricky to breathe. And there's something in my chest."

"Keep breathing," offered her mother, suddenly grasping at an immediate truth – the imperilled child needing support. "Keep breathing, Georgie."

*

Sam called the NHS number they were all being told to turn to instead of doctors and hospitals.

He came back to her bedside.

"OK. Maybe you *have* got it after all."

She looked at him with eyes that said: *Please don't kill me.*

It made him smile.

She felt something like panic prickle through her.

"Then you'll have to stay indoors with me. You mustn't spread it."

Her chest was pumping up and down rapidly. She could see from his expression that it was an alarming sight.

"Everything'll be all right," he said. "They said you've got to keep your temperature down."

"Mum," she said.

"I'll call her. Don't worry."

She couldn't speak now, had to calm her breathing.

He waited and watched.

"Tell her not to go out," she managed at last.

Sam nodded, tried to be reassuring but nothing could lessen her dread or the turmoil that was building in her chest.

*

"Georgie, darling. Are you OK? Sam told me you were unwell."

A night and day had passed in a fog of sleep and now it was night again. Georgie had woken with a start. The bed was damp and her skin clammy. She looked at the clock but her vision was blurry and she wasn't sure if it was midnight or two a.m.

"Mum, is everything OK?"

"I just wanted to call you before I forgot. I've found you the perfect dress-making pattern. Just right for your bust size. I'm going to order it for you."

Georgie kept to as few words as she could.

"Thank you. Now get to bed."

"Now?"

"Please, yes. Why are you up?"

"I'm sitting on my sofa very happily waiting for my cup of tea. Isn't that nice?"

Desperately tired, the fever rising, her voice fading, Georgie managed a simple: "Very nice."

"I just wanted to mention something else. Is that all right? While I've got you. Something I saw on the telly."

Georgie waited, entirely awake, monumentally tired.

"There were babies, you see."

"Babies?"

"It was a programme about something or other and there was a baby and it was so young that it was barely able to move and its mother came and scooped it up and…I can't remember what it was about really."

I'm always so stressed, thought Georgie. *Like I'm going to fly to pieces because of the pressure.*

Her mother had more to say: "They're utterly helpless, aren't they? They can't do a thing for themselves. They are human and everything is there – a brain, a heart – it's all there. And yet they can't do a thing for themselves. They're useless. Useless humans."

I'm so stressed.

"Thank God they've got others around them who can help them. Thank God for that, Georgie."

"I don't understand."

"Stupid, inert things. How horrible. How horrible to be alive and yet not even know it."

Georgie didn't understand whether to be angry or consoling. She couldn't prise any meaning from the moment.

"I'll go," said her mother quietly. And then the usual regret: "I'm sorry. I don't know why I'm telling you this. I thought you'd feel the same way. The same…the same outrage."

"Everything's fine," said Georgie. "We'll talk in the morning. Please don't worry. And Mama, you must stay at home from now on. Sam will bring you everything you need."

"Better go," said her mother, brightened. "Here's my tea. Don't worry about anything, sweetheart. It's all sorted. Got to go. Love you, love you."

As Georgie fell back against her pillows, the hard presence in her chest suddenly stinging and radiating, she craved sleep but couldn't bear the thought of it either.

In the morning, still awake, Sam looking down at her, visibly concerned and pressing out a number on his phone, she repeated what she'd been muttering through most of the night.

"Who made the tea? Sam – who made the bloody tea?"

3

People came and went, swathed in clear plastic. They would look in on her and inspect the tubes and the monitor and go away. But she wasn't aware of them, was unconscious, helpless, reduced to a useless thing. They could have done anything with her and she wouldn't have known about it. She was in a solid, dreamless sleep, unnatural, lumpen, like it had been visited on her. Which is exactly what it had been.

A week before, when she had been gasping for breath and sweating profusely, too frightened to ask what on earth was going on, a nurse had told her that they were going to give her a "little rest" so that the machine could breathe for her.

"Am I going to die?" she asked, quickly and between breaths.

A pause – an horrific pause – and then: "You're very poorly, Georgina. Your oxygen levels are low. We like them at 90. Yours are around 70 and dropping. You need help breathing."

"But will I die?" she spluttered once more. For clarity. This pin prick of a moment required clarity, not numbers.

That pause again. Why don't they just say it?

"You might."

At last.

The world was flying by at speed, the seen and the unseen world.

"But we've been putting people on ventilators for years. We're experts. Your body will have the best chance of recovering while something helps you with your breathing. We'll sedate you so you don't know what's going on – it's not very pleasant having a tube down your throat, after all. And we'll give you antibiotics and all kinds of things to give you the best chance."

And still the world rushed by, the past, the future, all a fearful, angry mass of somethings and nothings. Her child called out to her as though it were in her womb.

"We have to move fast."

She was asked to call her family and tell them what was going to happen but she could barely breathe, let alone form words. She didn't want them to hear her like that. She pushed her phone away.

"You really must," she was told. "They deserve to know."

"I love you," she told Sam between gasps. The nurse was holding the phone to Georgie's ear.

"Geeny," he said, and stopped.

"Tell Benjamin I love him."

"He's here with me. Hold on."

"Mum! Please just get better."

"OK," she answered. "OK."

And then she slept.

4

In the quiet of an afternoon, all you could hear was the child's pencils, picked up and dropped from the coffee table. The living room seemed to hum just perceptibly with her concentration. She drew, kneeling on the thick orange rug, and concentrated on filling the pads of cheap cartridge paper that her mother had left for her while she was out posting letters through strangers' doors. It filled an hour. Sometimes two. The girl would only ever look up from her work when the door opened and her mother returned. And always it felt like seeing her for the first time.

*

Beautiful Cherry Weston. Even her name was gorgeous.

All Georgie's life it had been the same. Everyone's eyes were on her mother. Including her own. When they looked away from the mother then the daughter felt affronted. There was nothing to see in the child, only in the adult. Such a lively, graceful, sunshine kind of person, not at all like other parents. Reed slim with long, restless legs that hooked together prettily at her ankles when she sat down, because – Georgie thought – it was the only way to stop her getting straight back up again. And not only did Georgie's mother have a wonderful name but she had also had a magical job. Cherry Weston had been a dancer, before Georgie was born. A real trained dancer. Georgie had seen photographs of her mother as a very young woman, a mane of permed curls frothing around her elfin face, her lithe body seemingly painted in pastel-coloured dancewear. And once or twice Georgie had even recognised Cherry Weston on TV in clips from those nostalgic re-runs of BBC Light Entertainment shows. There she was, pounding out routines with a group of fellow dancers, behind singers Georgie had never heard of and wasn't interested in. Georgie had grown up with stories of West End performances and summer variety shows – whatever *they* were – and had pored over publicity shots with grainy images of a young woman who looked so familiar with her enormous round eyes, high cheekbones and small, amused mouth. Cherry Weston, the dancer. And Georgie Weston, her daughter. What a perfect, perfect life they had of it with no one butting in, contentedly different from other families, living in a flat in Clapham, going out to eat, visiting markets and galleries. An annual three days in Whitstable. A winter in virtual hibernation. Staying up late, ignoring homework.

Men came occasionally and presumed to behave in a way that they owned Cherry. Georgie never liked to see it but knew that Cherry had no intention of being owned. She had been married once and it had ended two months before Georgie was born – "for reasons of outrageous fucking infidelity". He showed up occasionally, was studiously affectionate with his daughter, while his ex-wife stood by, looking over them, not with any pride or gratitude, but impatience. He was as supple and spare as Cherry – another dancer – but darker, with short, shiny black curls and solid brown eyebrows that the young Georgie thought were the most masculine things she'd ever seen, so unlike the fine pencil marks perched high on her mother's forehead. He was called Adam, a name which Georgie could never disassociate from the Bible, and she pictured him going home to his Eve, the only female irresistible – and conniving – enough to supplant Cherry Weston.

Georgie was eight when he stopped coming. Her mother showed her a picture of him standing beside a woman with straight black hair and wearing a thin pink dress with narrow straps.

"That's his new wife," she pointed out, letting the photograph drop onto the coffee table and moving on to other things.

"Will he forget about us?" asked Georgie, following her mother into the kitchen. "Now that he's got a new wife?"

Her mother raised those delicate arches. "Did he remember us much anyway?"

It was one of the very few times that the young Georgie heard her mother say anything self-pitying about their situation in regard to her father.

"Do you hate him now?" Georgie asked.

Her mother was taking milk from the fridge and turned around and looked her daughter in the eye.

"I will be forever grateful to that appalling loser for giving me the finest child in the world."

Partially apprised by then of the reproductive process, Georgie got what her mother meant by the fact that her father had *given* her. Less conversant with psycho-sexual gameplay, she wasn't clear why her mother would have had anything to do with a loser or why she still seemed to need to disparage him in light of his precious gift.

While Georgie was very young, Cherry worked part time as a doctor's receptionist. Money was sparse but she was at the primary school gates every afternoon which, she said, was the important thing. In the evenings for some years, she would supplement their income by stuffing photocopied fliers for local businesses into envelopes. She would do this for an hour or so in the living room, the radio on, and would rush out in her raincoat in the dark to put them through doors. Often, she came back to find Georgie drawing - Georgie drew at the coffee table, in bed, even in the bath – and they would discuss the pictures as forensically as they might the plot of a whodunnit. It thrilled the young girl to have these peculiar images that came rushing into her mind, often after hearing stories or watching TV, discussed with such tender kitchen-table erudition.

Georgie's favourite drawing projects – least liked by her mother – were what she called the telly innards. What went on behind the screen, she wondered? Cogs, electrodes, pulleys, bulbs, circuits and pendulums, a mad Heath Robinson mangle without her having ever seen a Heath Robinson drawing. Once the frame had been laid out with a ruler, she could spend days filling in the guts: snaking pipes, a wire mesh, tiny hammers, tracks, prisms, cylinders, small housings for lights, switches, clock faces. There was a logic to everything, Georgie having asked herself why one thing led to another, and another and yet another, and finally an image.

"You could hide a little mouse in there," her mother suggested. "Or a fairy. Yes, a TV fairy!"

Georgie was appalled.

"There's no air. They'd die. And they're not machines anyhow."

And so she'd stop, put the picture away, too self-conscious now, and produce a pony or castle instead. They could talk quite easily about ponies and castles. One day she'd learn how everything worked. Maybe her job would be to help make things function. Or to invent! Purpose was everything. To make things move and hum along happily due to her ingenuity was an elevating thought. But to draw just for the sake of it? No. Not interested.

"My talented little artist," said Cherry. "I'm so glad you have a vocation, too. Just like I did. A lifetime of self-expression. How wonderful."

"What's a vocation?" Georgie asked.

"A job you're born to do."

Was everyone born with a job already assigned to her? Did her mother come out of the womb pre-destined to dance and stuff envelopes? Georgie felt the first stirrings of panic, that sick feeling of knowing that you had it in you to disappoint your adult.

"You're exceptional," Cherry often told her. "Not ordinary. Some people are just born ordinary and can't escape it. You can't escape your specialness. It's who you are."

They moved – when Georgie was 10 – from Clapham into a downstairs flat in a small Victorian terrace house in East Dulwich.

The place was infested and filthy but while Georgie was at school each day, Cherry scrubbed and fumigated and slowly brought the place to rights. There was always a surprise waiting for Georgie when she got home: a freshly painted window sill, a new orange rug, a yellow kettle, one of her artworks, framed and on the living room wall.

"Beautiful original art and it costs me nothing," trilled Cherry.

"Will you teach me to dance?" asked Georgie, nervous about the prominence of her original art and wanting to widen her skills in case no other vocation emerged.

"Nah," said Cherry. "I'm finished with all that. It's a young woman's game. My knees don't like it."

"But it's your vocation!" exclaimed the girl, aghast. It was as good as a criminal act, wasn't it, to throw away a birthright? And her mother wasn't old. She was so bright and cheerful, so effortlessly stylish and easy-going and confident that she simply couldn't age. Not like other people, anyway.

Cherry bundled her daughter in her arms, smothered her tormented features so she didn't have to look at them, jollied away the distress. It was a special day, that day. There was something delicious to share with her girl.

"Come on, let's go for a walk."

It was a summer's evening and they had eaten dinner but it would still be light for ages and a walk wasn't unusual. They both loved to meander the streets, peer through the front windows of the rows of houses, glimpse family lives, children in front of television sets or doing their homework. People were always on sofas, Georgie noted, like survivors on life rafts, huddled together and safe. Some families ate their dinners there as well. Cherry hated that – not eating at tables – and Georgie was scandalised by the trays on laps and the automatic lifting of forks to mouths while eyes were trained elsewhere.

Cherry led them down one of the side streets to the road that ran parallel to the high street. They stopped before a shop. The sign across the front read *Annika* and there were two manikins in the window in white lace dresses, denim jackets and cowboy boots. One had a lace scarf knotted at the side of her face.

"Don't you love that look?" said Cherry.

Georgie shook her head.

"They look silly. Like they're all jumbled up."

"Denim and lace look lovely together. I'd prefer that dress with trainers, though. You know, baseball boots, but that's not the look she's going for."

Georgie didn't think either version was a sensible way to dress.

Her mother prodded up the corners of Georgie's mouth with her fingers.

"Give us a smile, love."

At that moment the door to the shop opened.

"Ah! This is the child."

Georgie pushed her mother's hands away, intensely embarrassed. A face lunged towards her, ragged white brows over sharp blue eyes. Metallic lips. Blonde curls framing a tanned face.

"Ha! She's nothing like you."

Georgie looked up to her mother for an explanation.

"I didn't know you'd be here this late," said Cherry to the stranger. "Stock-taking?"

The white-blonde woman turned her back on them while she locked the shop door.

"Correct. Lots of new things. Cream-colour dresses. Oh you should see them. Well…you will, anyhow."

The woman had an unusual, almost aggressive way of expressing herself. Her sentences came in neat blocks with spaces between. Georgie was old enough to know that she was foreign but had no idea beyond that what to make of her. The woman was in a get-up identical to the ones in the window, only her cowboy boots were pale blue with what looked like diamonds in a curling design on the top edge of each.

The three of them walked together for a while, the new woman declaiming in her precise word-blocks about taxes and import duties. Mysteries of the money variety. When they parted, the two women hugged as though they were friends, which came entirely as a surprise to the girl. The white-blonde woman stepped back and gave Georgie an over-long inspection before shaking her head.

"No," she said. "Nothing like you. See you tomorrow, Cherry. Early please. Lots of stock. It needs to be sorted out."

"See you, Annika. Don't worry. I'm looking forward to it."

Mother and daughter turned in the direction of their home. The sun was going down and graffiti on the shuttered shop fronts was as bright as medieval illuminated manuscripts.

"Bit scary, isn't she," grinned Cherry.

Georgie wanted to say so much – didn't like this Annika at all – but words didn't come. She felt her mother's arm slide across her back and herself being pulled in towards her. Always an awkward way to walk.

"My new boss. Starting at Annika's boutique tomorrow. I won't lie – I'm madly excited."

This was it? The next big adventure. Working in a shop?

What rubbish, thought Georgie. What total rubbish.

"She's German," explained her mother. "Very stylish – in her own way – and brings all these fab clothes over from the Continent and people seem to love them. It's lovely inside, that shop. Maybe after school tomorrow you can come and visit."

"I'll want to watch telly," said Georgie.

When they reached their front door, Cherry was talking about perms and how she was glad she didn't do that to her hair anymore, seeing how parched Annika's looked. She turned and smiled broadly at her daughter.

"Oh darling! I'm so excited. You don't seem very happy though. Are you cross?"

"No," said Georgie, her eyes filling with tears.

The front door was opened and then their flat door and then they were home, Georgie making straight for the TV.

"One day – sooner than you think – you'll go to art school and leave me here and I'll be alone. I need something, Georgie girl. I need to have things of my own. Business prospects. Do you know what that means?"

Georgie was looking at the television screen, her eyes now dry, her mouth flat and resolute. Art school? Where had that come from? Is that what her mother was planning for her?

As Cherry busied herself around the flat, Georgie felt a child's premonition of adulthood; saw conflict, experienced the sting of inevitable disagreement. The perfection of their life together might not – she now suddenly realised – be eternal. Her mother's intelligence not limitless, her own subservience not assured. Art school! There was no way that she would do anything as stupid as go to art school.

5

Cherry was remarkably good with money. Perhaps it was because of those financially difficult days when her baby girl had required her full attention and she'd given up dancing and had to think of more imaginative ways of maintaining them both. She was forever putting bits away. Even in the most straitened of times, she felt something had to be saved. Instinctively, she knew it would all count years down the line when she was old. It was just her way, to be thrifty and to save. She had been clever about saving when her daughter was young and they had lived simply. A child didn't need all that much in the way of possessions. A child needed love, food and company, in that order. Cherry supplied the first two more than adequately and Georgie didn't seem to need much of the last of them. Her mother learnt to cook very well, to sew and to present to the world two comfortable-seeming, well-dressed, healthy members of society. And all the while she saved and saved and when Georgie was fourteen Cherry bought their first home – a large, two-bedroomed flat on the first floor of a Victorian villa in Nunhead. Sheltering quietly under a horse chestnut, the house was dark, and a little morose to Georgie's mind. But as her mother pointed out, a piece of it was theirs and it was a more fitting home for a working woman and her gifted artist daughter.

Cherry was also a valuable business partner to Annika Walter. Within a year of having joined the boutique, she and Annika were discussing expansion – not with more shops but with a different approach to making money. Annika's stock – the pastel colours, washed-out denims and rhinestones, considered very continental and glamorous – had won her a substantial following and customer loyalty. The women initially wondered if more outlets might be the answer, but Cherry was worried about the cost of extra staffing and increased overheads and administration.

"We must keep as much of the labour to ourselves," she told her partner. "Let other people do the selling." In fact, the idea to be fashion buyers and importers came from a late-night conversation between Cherry and her teenage daughter, which was always a fertile ground for ideas. Georgie had simply asked her mother: "Can you be arsed, Mum? Do you really want to spend hours chatting to dull women who then don't buy anything in the end?"

Chatting to other women was usually a pleasure, as it happened, but Georgie was right, it was no way to run a business. A year later, while Georgie was busily trying to survive in her South London comprehensive, Annika Walter and Cherry Weston closed the boutique and settled into their tiny office in Annika's garage from where they ran their fashion import firm – Walter & Weston. Annika travelled to Germany to choose stock while Cherry made contacts among the clothes shops of South East England and made deals over white lace jackets and pink stilettos. They didn't make a fortune but at least Cherry and Georgie got their own home and Cherry enjoyed more than a decade of enormous fun in retail.

Beautiful Cherry Weston. Once a dancer, now a businesswoman. Well-dressed – though never in the German denim and rhinestones – and devoted to her daughter. The best friendship, the best times.

Nothing stays the same. Love can't. Children simply won't. Despite owning a home and living comfortably, neither mother nor daughter was a hundred per cent happy as such. Cherry because she was ageing and alone, Georgie because she wanted to age and to be alone.

How quickly it came, the revision of their relationship. Not over a long time, but suddenly. A restive daughter, an agitated mother. By her late teens Georgie was wholly possessed by an easily-provoked and universal irritation. She was oppressed by boredom, disgusted by familiarity, and associated both with her mother. Cherry's in-jokes, her views, her tastes, her clothes, her friends, all seemed to stoke her daughter's hyper-sensitivity. Once they had loved to visit charity shops together and find hidden bargains, now mother chided daughter for wearing what she called rags and the daughter was critical of her mother's embarrassingly young appearance.

Cherry had her own sensitivities. She passed through the shock of dealing with an irrational teenager without being able to see beyond it. Present antagonism was such a contrast to past contentedness, that it didn't occur to either that this might just be a phase, a grisly passage for both to somewhere new and different. For Cherry, her daughter's taciturnity seemed to presage a lonely old age and now was not the time to be shoved aside and forgotten. She felt she needed to assert herself. Cherry not only insisted that her daughter go to art school but made the added mistake of suggesting she stay in London and live at home, to save money. Georgie had retorted that it wasn't *healthy*, mother and daughter living together and that she couldn't bear the idea.

"Ach it happens in all animals," said Annika. "While the kitten is small, the mother loves it. When the kitten grows, there is no room for two adult female cats. They must be put apart for the good of everybody."

Cherry, bloody-minded in her late forties and wanting to remind her daughter of her treachery at every moment, recited Annika's words to her.

"What are you saying? That I should have stayed your kitten?"

"No," said her mother, suddenly sounding so forlorn. "I'm saying that somewhere inside *I* wanted to stay a kitten forever and was hoping you'd be the cat."

Not now, Georgie had thought. I won't tell you what you want to hear. Go and sell your stupid clothes and leave me alone.

*

From the very start of that evening, Cherry had been artful and impish.

Georgie instantly regretted being there and having brought her new boyfriend and fellow-student to her home.

"Rod!" Cherry had guffawed. "Really? That's a name and a half."

"God. You're going to get all sexual, aren't you?" Georgie's spirit plummeted. They were in the kitchen, while Rod was at the dinner table, waiting.

Cherry had made a lasagne – her entertaining dish – and Georgie was watching her mother mix a salad dressing and pour it over the washed leaves.

"I *am* sexual," said Cherry. "And so are you. You should let yourself go, darling. Get a bit saucy with him. He'd probably love it."

"Saucy! Who says saucy anymore? You're such an embarrassment."

Rod was charming all evening, talked mainly about movies and his intention to work in them. Cherry had listened, rapt, to his ardent views on the British film industry and had encouraged him, as she put it, to *thrust* his way through life.

Georgie waited, mostly silent and on the lookout, ready to step in with conversational distractions. She had them all ready.

When the main course was over her mother stood up and threw her napkin on the table.

"Pudding!" she declared. "Oh, I'm having such a lovely time. I don't see young people much these days. I always hoped Georgie would bring home all her school friends but – if she had any – she didn't want to share them with me. I understand."

She left the room and Georgie turned to see an astonished expression on Rod's face.

"Ouch," he said. "I thought you said you two got on really well?"

Had she said that to him? She didn't even remember mentioning her mother in detail. They did get on. They were close. Only not as close as they used to be. That was natural, surely. For a child to grow up and grow away. And Georgie so desperately wanted to get away.

Cherry placed four ramekins of chocolate mousse on the table.

"One extra for a hearty male appetite," she said.

Cherry made chocolate mousse very well – it was her daughter's favourite of her mother's upmarket concoctions – and Georgie watched Rod's face for approval.

"Fabulous," he said, after finishing the second pot.

Cherry grinned at the pair of them.

"I'm afraid there's only one double bed and that's mine," she said. "I'm happy to lend it for the night. If that's more…useful."

Rod held up his hands.

"Oh no, no. I'm not staying. Please don't worry."

Cherry made a fuss about him not staying. She'd assumed he would be. Georgie had made the same assumption.

"I've got a big project to finish tonight. A set design. I'm going straight to the studio from here."

"Are you?" asked Georgie faintly. Her mother was talking over her already.

"I never went to college of course, Rod," she was saying. "Though I did train at a dance school."

"That's the same thing," he shrugged.

"I don't think so."

"It is, Mum," said Georgie. "It's exactly the same thing. It's higher education of a sort."

"*Of a sort*," Cherry scoffed. "Thank you, my love."

"I meant it in a good way." Georgie could feel the quality of the air between them degrading. She was desperate now to appease, terrified of anything like a disagreement arriving at what was so nearly the end of the evening. "And you went to a good school. You always say so."

"I have skills," said Cherry with a sharp nod to bring home the point.

"Dancing, that sort of thing?" asked Rod affably.

"Dancing, acting, singing. But other skills as well. Life skills. I had to acquire them."

"Very important," he agreed.

Georgie looked on, frozen.

"And then," said her mother, "yet another layer of skills. My own special skills."

"Really?" said Rod, returning her grin. "And what are those?"

Georgie felt her blood stop in her veins.

Why on earth would you ask!

Cherry's very thin brows hoisted themselves high up into her hairline. "I can bring myself to orgasm just by thinking about it and I can mortally embarrass my daughter with only a few choice words." And she had leaned into the poor, speechless young man and added: "I've just done one of those things this minute and I'll let you guess which one."

*

"I hate you," Georgie said in the kitchen. Rod had left. Not hurriedly or awkwardly but – clearly as he'd always planned – once he'd eaten the free dinner and put up with the conversation.

"Oh get off your high horse."

Cherry was moving plates dejectedly from one surface to another, getting nowhere. "Young people are obsessed with sex. If he's going to work in the film industry, he'll appreciate the line. I wouldn't be at all surprised if it surfaces in a movie in ten years' time."

This was where it ended. Georgie would leave as well and let this sad middle-aged woman wallow in her nastiness. That's what she thought, although she felt very uncomfortable thinking it. All the same, she had to strike a blow now, to end things and to move on with a clear path ahead.

"You were wrong about me. So wrong."

Cherry didn't even look up from the disconsolate dance of plates and cutlery.

"You pushed me in the direction you wanted me to go."

"What are you talking about?" her mother mumbled.

"Art. Fucking art."

Finally, Cherry looked up from the plates, at a loss.

"I don't know what you're on about."

"I'm packing it in. I hate it. It was never right for me. You made me do it."

As the news sank in, so Cherry seemed to crumble. She was failing to conjure the right words. Georgie took hold of the advantage.

"My supervisor thinks the same thing. You know what he said to me yesterday? 'You're a fabulous drawer, Georgina. You are a draftswoman. But you're no artist.' He thought he was breaking my heart. But he wasn't. Finally, someone was letting me off the hook. This year has been awful. And it's your fault."

"Georgie…"

"I never wanted to do it."

"Your pictures. You have a gift."

"I don't! *I* knew I didn't so why did you?"

"You think I can't spot talent?"

"Not in me you can't. Evidently."

"Then what are you going to do?"

Georgie was suddenly tired of the conversation and left the kitchen. She sat for a while on the sofa while her mother washed up. She wasn't going to help. Let her do all the labour. She'd ruined the evening anyway. Eventually, the clattering in the kitchen came to an end and Cherry arrived on the sofa beside her daughter. She was rubbing cream into her hands and looking into the distance.

"What are you going to do?"

Should she tell her? There was always a risk in opening up to Cherry when she was in such a self-pitying mood. She could turn everything around on a sixpence. But then she would want the best for her daughter, wouldn't she? She'd want to be kept apprised of her decision.

"I'm going to switch to law."

There was a silence which Georgie took to be serious contemplation – until she heard the wheezes of held-back laughter.

Cherry let it all out at last. "Darling, come on! You're the least lawyerly person I know."

To which Georgie sprung up from the sofa.

"Oh fuck off, you evil old bat."

She left the room to the sounds of her mother's laughter and requests for her to come back and "talk it through".

"There's nothing to talk about," she shouted from her bedroom. And there wasn't.

*

Three years of a law degree, a further year at law school and then one year in-house at a charity before Georgina – now calling herself Gina – could do what she had longed to do for most of her conscious life: lose herself in the details. She set out on a Whitehall apprenticeship, moving from department to department, acquiring casework almost at once. Very quickly she moved on from casework to settle among the select few who advised on drafting policy. And there she stayed. She started her thirties satisfied that she was who she should be, valuable, independent, earning well and immersed entirely in the absorbing task of making law. The past had brought her here but that didn't mean that she had to dwell on it. And who knew what the future might bring (how uncomfortable to think that it might bring anything different). The now mattered and her most rewarding times were spent unravelling and unknotting, solving and clarifying.

What – she wondered – had her mother been talking about when she claimed she was lonely? Solitariness stretched before Georgie like the impossible beauty of a trail of midsummer stars.

6

When she woke it was because the machine had abandoned her. She opened her eyes to find two nurses looking down on her and, far from feeling reassured, she felt forsaken. She was on her own. It was as though a god who had shielded her and held her close to him, had fled and left her soul vacant.

Georgie gasped and felt her eyes widen. The pain in her throat was almost too shockingly intense for her to know how to respond to it. It was just there, in all its freshly scraped rawness and she'd never had to deal with anything like it before.

The nurses applauded and told her how clever she was to be breathing for herself.

"You've done it!" said one through a white mask and plastic visor. "You're one of the special ones. Well done, Georgina."

She didn't feel remotely special. She was not even sure where she was or why she was there. So, she closed her eyes and went back to sleep.

This time her sleep was not the dead kind, not the slamming of a door, but something far more interesting and familiar. This time she saw things.

She saw the blue blurs of plastic-clad humans moving about in the distance and she was convinced that she was in space, hovering outside a ship, the blue people inside the ship and getting on with their work. They couldn't hear her and didn't know she was out there. She would wave if she could but her damn space suit was too heavy and she couldn't lift her arms. And so, she kept on drifting, attempting now and again to get their attention, knowing of course that in space no one can hear you scream.

At one point she passed George Clooney and at another Sandra Bullock, both in their space suits.

They were busy, too, and though she tried to speak to them, no words came out. She had to accept the fact that she would go on drifting forever, comfortably, deadened, powerless to alter her course or even to get noticed. She felt perhaps that she was awake but that everyone else was half asleep and not quite with it.

*

The curtains were closed around the bed beside hers. But she knew what was going on. A very large woman was being turned over to lie on her stomach. It needed four nurses, three male, one female, to accomplish the task and it was taking an age. The nurses had psyched themselves up, counted themselves in, and one had groaned audibly as he helped lift and shift. The patient made no noise at all.

Georgie had a mask over her mouth and was breathing for herself, shallowly and rapidly, but most definitely for herself. The woman who was being turned could barely breathe at all. They had taken her off the ventilator too early, Georgie had heard one of the nurses say. The other nurse had said: "Don't beat yourself up. It wasn't our call."

She hadn't understood. Georgie just watched and, when she didn't watch, she slept.

One of the things she liked to watch was her chest as it rose and fell like some over-sensitive engine. If she tried to move, then the engine sped up. If she counted to a hundred slowly and steadily, then the engine slowed a little. If she tried to talk then she would cough and coughing exhausted her and the engine would go berserk.

There was a moment of collective silent triumph – Georgie sensed it – once her fellow-patient was overturned and the curtain was yanked open. One of the nurses remained to rearrange wires around the patient, two left down the corridor, and the last turned to Georgie.

She said something but it was uttered from under a mask and visor and Georgie couldn't care less what was said and so didn't bother to show anything in response. The nurse looked into Georgie's eyes. Georgie stared back into two flecked brown irises. She was looking forward to her dreams. Her dreams were captivating and strange and were triggered by the merest glimpse of anything new – for example, two flecked brown irises.

The nurse checked the fluids running into Georgie's arm and shook her head. She squeezed the pouch and then clapped. Georgie merely stared over the top of her mask. She wasn't able to smile because it took too much effort and dislodged things.

And so the dreams arrived and this time they were populated with children, her son as a boy in the playground with his friends, climbing up a slide the wrong way, stopping at the top to wave down at her. Then she was back in the little kitchen of her childhood, her mother searching through cupboards, laughing as she did so, telling her that there was nothing but babies in the cupboard, delighted in seeing them squirming and gurgling good-naturedly inside.

"But what will we eat?" asked Georgie.

Her mother gave her one of her conspiratorial looks, with arched brows and a malevolent smile.

When she awoke, perhaps moments later, perhaps days, her throat felt so dry and her hips so sore that tears arrived along with consciousness.

"Now then," said a voice beside her.

Georgie tried to turn her head but couldn't and so she blinked away her dampness and nodded a hello.

It was a new nurse, a male one, or possibly a doctor, they all dressed the same way, with scrubs and caps and masks and aprons and visors.

"We think it's time you went into the recovery ward. Your signs are very good. This isn't the right place for you anymore."

She felt her chest rise and fall, rise and fall.

"Don't worry. You'll receive excellent care. We can monitor you just as well. And you can sit up a bit better there and phone your folks. Yeah? Great."

As he leaned over her, his name badge swung in front of her eyes. *Dr Efren Benjamin.*

"I have a Benjamin," she said. It was the first time she had heard her voice in weeks. She didn't recognise it.

No response. Dr Benjamin looked at her fluid pouch, frowned, squeezed it, then said "yay" and left.

She wasn't sure now if she'd actually spoken. She had a son, had she? How funny. Or no son – or two? Many children? And a husband. He had always wanted a brood of kids. Yes, that was right. Lots of children. Had she delivered? Should she ask the doctor? Would he like to know? She suddenly saw all the squirming babies in the wall cupboards. Is that where one got them from?

She fell asleep.

*

She opened a magazine and there was a lion's face inside. It was moving, panting. It dominated the double page and its amber eyes looked back at her solidly and defiantly. She was mesmerised but frightened, convinced it was going to jump.

"Don't make friends with it," said a voice from somewhere. "Don't let it know you're afraid."

7

Only an hour before, he had been nothing more than another man in a dark suit, one of a group poring over her amendments to a new bill, taking notes before reporting back to his minister. She hadn't even realised that she'd noticed him. But she must have because there he was, standing on the concourse beside her at Charing Cross and – dammit – catching her eye. A curt hello and an exchanged nod. But then they were sitting beside each other on the train and had no choice but to elongate the pain of sociability.

By the time he got off, she wished he hadn't. The way they had spoken to each other – the ease of it – felt like coming across a fellow countryman in a foreign land. A relief. They seemed bemused to be finding each other so attractive, trying the idea for size, getting used to it surprisingly quickly.

"Samuel Greenfield," she said. "You sound like a character in a Thomas Hardy novel. Are we allowed to call you Sam?"

"I like Samuel," he said. "Too many things are shortened."

At 36, he was four years older than her. She had always thought she liked boyish men but Samuel Greenfield was not at all frivolous or youthful. He came across as thoughtful and practical and, well, *grown-up*. She guessed that this conversation was as playful as he got.

"Anyway, what's Gina short for? Regina?"

"Regina! Good God, no. I'm Georgina."

After consideration he decided that in her case the shortened form was slightly preferable. "Not that there's anything wrong with Georgina, of course. I just like Gina."

"My mother calls me Georgie."

He shook his head. "You're not a Georgie," he said.

Maybe not to you.

It turned out that he *could* be a little playful, but only with the woman he married and only in private. She moved into his flat a year after that meeting and they married three months after that. When they expressed their love for each other, they did it almost as though they were slipping a clause sneakily into an otherwise perfectly workable agreement, so that she might say: "The fact that I love you, means that I can't imagine having an affair," or he might explain away her sadness when he went off on work trips abroad with the logic that that's what happened when two people, *who loved each other*, had to be apart for any length of time. It was love, presumably, that let the transgression of calling him Sam slip by unremarked. It was one of the many ways, he marvelled aloud, in which she softened him and made him more genial to others as well.

They drove around Greater London like a pair of holidaying pensioners on country roads. It was their post-work and weekend entertainment, especially in the summer when the long evenings begged to be used and the flat felt so stifling. They were drawn to the south of the city, crossed out of London into Surrey or Kent. As the evening sun was going down, they would pass through what still felt like villages but were far from remote, historically interesting locations marred by the very roads that were providing their adventures. They felt nothing but wonder at the way others lived outside London and explored suburbia with a kind of limited amazement that humans could exist like this, quietly, unremarkably, with nothing but neighbours, many, many neighbours. What they were doing, of course, was finding somewhere to live and to have a family, though neither said it out loud. It was understood.

In the end, their odyssey led them to a total surprise, a place that wasn't a village or a conurbation, didn't feel outside London and yet didn't feel like London either. It was just a street but a street that was so self-contained that everything beyond appeared to be detached and poorer, cheaper and plainer. They had left Chislehurst and were heading towards Orpington when they turned off the carriageway on a whim into the tree-guarded entrance to a road named The Brake. It was a cul-de-sac of very large mock-Tudor detached houses, dating probably from the twenties, Sam guessed, immaculate, with sloping lawns to the front, mature shrubs in well-kept beds, imposing family homes that were lovingly cared for in a broad avenue of old trees. They found it when it was at its most beautiful and tranquil in late summer, sunlight scattered through the leaves, neighbours meeting at front doors, an exclusivity and secrecy about the place that called to both of them powerfully. When those houses were built, they mused aloud, they were aimed at moneyed professionals who dreamt of their own little moated Tudor granges but within striking distance of their jobs in the City. The moats were actually 360 degrees of lawn and the granges were rather more modern and water-tight than their ancient models, but the sense of seclusion and uncommonness made the place a rare treasure in the eyes of certain types. By the time Georgie and Sam came across it, the residents were a mix of relatively wealthy middle-class families, like them, who wanted space and like-mindedness, and older, slightly more bohemian couples, who had bought their homes in the seventies when the houses were laughably old-fashioned and cheap.

Nothing else after that came close to the perfection of the place. The vision of The Brake remained before their eyes like the final prize in a feverish sprint that might well turn into a marathon. "When we live in The Brake..." was a regular conversation-starter. It took four years for them to secure a house for themselves and in that time they planned for it as though it were an inevitability. What neither of them guessed as they exchanged on their lovely four-bedroomed haven, was that Georgie was pregnant – only a few weeks – and that they were not only acquiring their dream home but also the beginnings of a family.

Step outside The Brake, go along the main road, and you were greeted by a housing estate of squat, unremarkable replicated boxes, exactly the ugly world that made Sam wince but that didn't need to be visited or acknowledged. They could, if you were determined, be avoided altogether. Sam would take the car to the station to get a train to Town for work and, later, when Georgie went back to Whitehall, she went with him.

From the moment they arrived in The Brake, Georgie realised what she truly hated. She hated having to move home. She would try never do it again. She and Sam were so firmly tied to the place, that it wasn't just an impressive house, but an acknowledgment of their mortality. This was the location where – Georgie felt convinced – she would contentedly grow old and die.

8

Georgie was irritated and embarrassed by pregnancy. She was at her sweetly funniest – her mother thought – as she negotiated her way through the many doubts and anxieties of impending motherhood. Nothing seemed to be going as she planned – not least the expected blooming – and she let Cherry see her at her most vulnerable. Her mother was touched by her daughter's sudden candour, her unspoken appeal for support, which swept aside the frostiness that had existed between the two during Georgie's twenties.

In fact, the stand-off had been losing its chill for some time now, helped along bit by bit by the occasional spontaneous phonecall and sharing of domestic news. They had never entirely abandoned each other, leaving in place a thread of communication, but their love, which had been so tested, was changing. Neither wanted to depend on the other and yet each wanted to care for the other – without the other even knowing it. Georgie was still impatient and often a little brusque with her mother, but Cherry had acquired a doting tolerance which meant that her daughter's barbs never sank deep. It surprised her how little she cared to fight, how pointless it was to take offence and let anything come between them. If conflict ever rumbled distantly, she saw it off at once. The loneliness she had dreaded as she approached her late middle age, turned out to be something far more positive. She felt increasingly unhindered and independent. And so, when Georgie turned to her mother for support in the first queasy trimester, it was easy for Cherry to put aside all other considerations and be there for her girl. The time for trivial gripes and recriminations between them was over. Neither of them was a kitten anymore.

Walters & Weston had been sold a while back. The craze for the romantic cowgirl had long expired and Cherry and Annika had stepped across from German denim to Italian shoes and handbags before devoting the company's last two years to importing Egyptian cotton pyjamas for high-end Knightsbridge boutiques. The business partners were both sixty now and driven by a desire for other adventures beyond fabrics and fashion. Annika had got it into her head that she wanted to write self-help books for women in business and Cherry…she was going to be a grandmother and had a suspicion that she would need to be on hand.

Cherry hesitated before she put the big question before her daughter. Georgie was lying on the sofa in the large kitchen diner at the back of the house. The French windows were open even though it was only March and the temperature was on the point of icy. Georgie said she didn't feel the cold anymore and wanted air.

"I don't know how you'd feel about this, Georgie girl, but I could move closer to you, to be of help. You plan to go back to work and…"

"Damn right I do!"

"Well, why pay someone else to look after the baby when I could do it for nothing?"

"I can't ask that of you, Mum," said Georgie, dearly wanting to ask her mother exactly that. "What would you do with the Nunhead flat? And these houses don't come up for sale very often, let alone for rent. Oh, you mean live *with* us? I don't know what Sam would say…"

"No, darling, no." Cherry was finding Georgie delightfully helpless. It melted her heart. "Have you looked beyond your street? There are tonnes of houses out there. Little ones, the perfect size for single grannies."

Georgie flinched.

"You mean the estate?"

"Why not? I could buy three of those houses from the sale of the Nunhead flat. I'll just get the one, of course, and the money I save can go to you or the little one once I've gone."

Two awfulnesses there. The thought of her chic, urbane mother living in a dismal housing estate and the notion of her ever dying. Yet one wonderfulness: to have her nearby.

"And you know I've only one ambition left – to have a nice red front door," said Cherry and it felt to Georgie, trying out the idea, that, yes, she could see herself knocking on a neat red front door and it opening to her mother's smiling face. And competent arms.

It all happened surprisingly quickly and gave mother and daughter a sense of a new start. Cherry was thrilled to be of help and not a little excited about buying a house. Georgie was relieved that she could defer to someone wiser when it came to caring for a small human, someone to whom it came more naturally. In the first months of Benjamin's life, the two women were on an expedition and discovered unknown depths of pragmatism, resourcefulness and honest, useful love. Georgie was so shell-shocked by the process of switching from non-parent to parent, that she couldn't let her mother out of her sight. But Cherry was so tactful about it all. When Sam came home from work, Cherry would step back with a friendly "over to you". Georgie was relieved and proud to find that a new respect was growing between her husband and his mother-in-law and that she might be the cause of it.

When not carrying around a wailing baby or cooking for a tired new mother and father, Cherry was busily arranging her house move. Benjamin was nearly four months old when she found the right little broken-down box and pushing nine months when she moved into it. At weekends, the baby stayed at home with his father while Georgie went over to the house to watch her mother smash the old patio, and to help her dig up the weedy turf and lay a new paved garden. While the plasterer and electrician came to make good the walls and wiring, Cherry stayed briefly in the loft room at the house in The Brake. Mother and daughter planned the paint colours and the garden design but, in reality, it was Cherry who had the inspired though workable ideas and Cherry who relished knocking the house into shape. She very gingerly released money from her savings for a new roof and for a damp course, but otherwise she worked on an impressively tight budget. She did the decorating herself, painted the rooms in tasteful muted shades of grey, cream and mauve. She found curtains, rugs and kitchenware that was of the highest quality and yet inexpensive. From the reclamation yard in Lewisham, she bought a sofa that simply needed steam-cleaning to make good again. She insisted on keeping the dated fitted kitchen but in a week somehow managed to transform it into a clean, white, homely and pristine space.

The house consisted of a living room at the front and a kitchen and downstairs toilet at the back. Upstairs was a miniscule bathroom and two bedrooms: one small, one very small. The bigger bedroom, her mother's, overlooked the street and not the garden which Georgie thought scandalous. Her mother told her she liked to hear goings-on outside and to feel she was part of a community. And she did, remarkably, find a handful of relatively genteel friends locally, mainly retired couples who thought they were taking her under their wing, convinced that she had fallen on hard times. Why else would such a well-heeled former businesswoman be living in an ex-council house on the middle of an estate?

"I don't need much space," she told Georgie's neighbours once, with Georgie hovering nearby. "And I don't care what's outside the front door. It doesn't bother me. Besides, it's a very friendly neighbourhood, mine."

She had leaned in for the clincher: "Why risk my money in property at the moment? At least I know it's doing very well in a high-yield savings account, ready for Georgie or Benjamin or whoever will eventually benefit from it."

Georgie had remonstrated with her mother afterwards.

"Mum, really, you shouldn't talk to people about money. It sounds odd."

"Nonsense," said Cherry. "People love talking about money. It's just that they've been brought up not to."

"Because it's vulgar and awkward."

"Vulgar indeed!" muttered her mother. Not offended. They never managed to touch raw nerves these days, never set each other off in a sulk. Things were in perspective now. They were not living entirely for themselves but for another, an energetic little boy who was deeply attached to both of them and had to be attended to all the time. There was a sense of years passing on. Maybe it was because he grew so rapidly, was in such a rush to talk and run and make and understand. As he grew, so the two women in his life kept adjusting themselves to his needs, changing the way they spoke to him, acquainting themselves with all his interests, finding infinite amounts of time to listen to him. There was not the slightest anxiety about it all ending – one day he'd go off to university, would fall in love and move away – and that was fine because they had each other.

*

"Men are such simple creatures," said Cherry. She was dressing Benjamin, who had his arms tightly round her neck, while speaking to Georgie. "Little boys need sleep and food. Young men need sleep, food and sex. And older men just need sleep."

Georgie often stopped what she was doing to admire that very natural knot of grandson and grandmother. They were forever clinging on to each other, as though letting go might be perilous. The three of them were going through the usual brief flurry of morning madness as Georgie got ready for work and handed her child over to her mother. Handed? Returned.

"That's sexist nonsense," she said. "Females don't need much to keep them happy either."

Her mother hadn't even paused in pulling up Benjamin's trousers. "Didn't you know? Females are never happy."

The problem with growing up as the single child of a single parent, Georgie often thought, was the fact that you only have one source of aphorisms and they become lodged for life.

*

"Look," said her mother. "I can't seem to part with them. Do you remember? You hated them."

They were in Cherry's kitchen, Georgie at the little two-person table with her cup of tea and some toast. Cherry had placed a neat, folded stack of fabric on the table. Pinks, yellows and creams, all in a pale blur.

"My old curtains," said Georgie.

"From the East Dulwich flat," said her mother.

Georgie pressed a hand down on the top of the pile. Chalky, laundered fabric, not musty at all, but fresh and well-aired.

"I love them. Isn't that funny! Is that just nostalgia or can I genuinely see the beauty of such things now in a way I couldn't then?"

"Tastes change," said Cherry, pulling out a chair. "People my age loved Laura Ashley then." The two women stared at the neat block of folded fabric and lost themselves in the faded colours and vague floral pattern.

"I can see them now in your bedroom," said Cherry fondly. "Near your bed. That Escher-type picture pinned on the wall beside them."

"I remember!"

"They're precious to me. But I'll put them in the spare bedroom anyway. They need to be hung, not packed away as a museum piece. Unless you can use them?"

Georgie was back in her old bedroom, the tiny bright space in a tiny, busy flat. Her mother had slept on the fold-out sofa in the living room. Had they really lived in such a small and compromised way? On top of each other? The coffee table had been the centre of their world, where Georgie drew her pictures, her pencils lying beside her mother's steaming coffee mug, an inevitable fashion magazine lying open, the spine rucked up like a tent.

"They wouldn't look right in my place," she said quietly.

"Then I'll keep them and use them. That back bedroom could be so pretty if kept plain and a bit Shaker. And do you know what? I've noticed that if you lean out of that window far enough you can see the tops of the trees in your street. I love that."

"Me too," said Georgie, her voice as dreamy and faint as the washed-out colours beneath her fingers.

*

They walked. Greeted each other in the same place – the white lock-ups at the end of Cherry's road – and turned toward the main road, could hear the traffic all the while, before veering off towards the town centre, eventually leaving that road as well, cutting through the cemetery. A narrow path ran down the side of it and they would have to walk one behind the other for a few minutes.

From behind, Cherry in her seventies was exactly as she always had been, slim, neck erect, elegant shoulders, sleek hair – worn in a turned-under bob for the past thirty years – long legs. Always in heels – very slight heels for walking – but always some ankle-displaying elevation.

It was just her face that was a little different these days. A little inward-looking, concerned. That's what caused the few lines, the concern. Georgie couldn't bear to add to her concerns, or to contribute a new line.

They walked four days a week. The rest of the time Georgie was either working or having to be with her family. When her son had been little they had walked as a threesome – that's why their destination was the park gardens, so that Benjamin could play on the swings, while Georgie and Cherry sat together watching and chatting.

They carried on walking when he started nursery and then primary school and secondary. And they were still walking when he left for university, both of them full of speculation about the structure of his day, his changing character, his love life.

Two women walking. One elegant and slim, the other rounder in the back and shoulders. Bigger, a little more gauche. But they were close. Evidently, so close. What did people think? They didn't think anything, because Georgina Greenfield and Cherry Weston were, despite everything, old enough to be unremarkable, middle-aged and old-aged, minding their own business, unknown, undistinguished, a suburban pair in a bland suburban setting. Maybe affection. You could sense love, there. Easy, uncomplicated, arrived-at love.

9

A short but strongly built young woman introduced herself as Naomi and said she was a hospital physiotherapist.

"They should just call us therapists," she confided. "At the moment that's what we are. We listen and we help. And we chat a lot. It's not just about walking again."

Georgie clamped her eyes shut to squeeze away the latest dream, then opened them and focused on the girl's perfect complexion. There was a tiny tattoo of a daisy just beneath her left ear.

"It's good that you were only on the ventilator a really short time. It should make your recovery that bit faster," she said.

Georgie tried to smile and found she could.

"Let's do some basic exercises, shall we?" suggested Naomi.

The exercises turned out to be lifting shoulders and dropping them, breathing slowly and a bit of head-tilting.

"We'll have you running a marathon soon," beamed Naomi, which was presumably what she said to everyone as limp as Georgie was.

"I've got a sore throat," said Georgie with some tragedy.

"Let's get you some water," soothed the physio and disappeared.

It seemed like she was away for a lifetime. At one point, Georgie – convinced she was dying of a rapidly constricting throat – thought she could hear the young woman laughing with colleagues somewhere further up the corridor.

Naomi returned with water and watched Georgie sip it wincingly.

"Aww," she said.

*

"Naomi," asked Georgie. "Could you ask someone if I could have a bit more jelly. It doesn't matter, does it, if I ask for more jelly?"

Naomi had become for Georgie exactly what she'd predicted – a supportive companion who was increasingly longed for. Under the guise of getting Georgie to walk again, Naomi could improve her mood as well and let her talk more and more about a world outside that for around a month had receded into something like a forgotten childhood.

"You can have a million jellies," said Naomi. "Eat what you like. No one will recognise you, you're that thin."

"No bad thing," agreed Georgie.

"Think of all the calories you can unleash now. You've got a free pass to eat what you like."

"I think I've had that free pass all my life."

"Aww," said Naomi, who utilised this catch-all response when she wasn't quite sure whether she should be laughing at, with or despite someone else following an unexpected comment.

"I'm going to call my husband in a moment," said Georgie.

"That's nice."

"He won't know what hit him."

"Aww."

Georgie had called Sam once before and had meant it to be a wonderful surprise but had choked up as soon as she heard his voice and so their conversation had been brief and tearful on both sides with Sam asking her repeatedly how she was feeling and with her replying each time with a shaky "all right".

"I've got lots of things to ask," she told her physio.

"You just take it slowly," counselled Naomi. "Don't get yourself too excited. I want all your energy going into standing up and taking some steps today."

Georgie focused on the tattoo on Naomi's right wrist. It read *love*. Once she would have found it unbearably mawkish. Now just the sight of it filled her heart with awe for the bountiful care and affection in others.

"Will you get to have a little chat with your son?" asked the nurse.

"I think so. He's living at home again. Everyone's locked down."

"Aww," said Naomi. "It's very different outside. You wouldn't recognise it. Really quiet."

Georgie couldn't imagine the outside world anyway. It had gone.

"The thing is," started Naomi, as though she were picking up on a conversation that Georgie had blinked and missed, "you'll have some down days. It's not your fault. Anyone coming off a ventilator feels a bit light-headed at first but then you drop a little. It can mess with your head a bit, intubation. It's quite normal. Anyway, you were on it for such a short time that it probably won't happen. Or not much. I'm here if you're unhappy, don't forget that."

"I'm all right," said Georgie.

"Just take it slowly. Recovery will take a long time. Much longer than you think. Your lungs are pretty battered for a start."

"I've got things to do."

"Oh yeah? Like what?"

Georgie's eyes filled at once. She wasn't sure at all about what she wanted and was surprised that she'd said it. She wanted to be left alone largely, but beyond that her other longing was to smell that space in her husband's neck beneath his ear. It was the smell she went to sleep to and she actually missed it – missed a smell! – even if she couldn't picture the person it came from.

Her other longing came in and out of focus. It was a yearning for Cherry, but it came with a feeling of exhaustion. She had let her mother down by being ill and now she didn't have the strength to work out how she could be of any use to her again. Cherry Weston. She said the name to herself, as though she were remembering an old friend, and when she said it she saw her childhood curtains hanging at the back bedroom window. Nothing beyond. Her mother trapped in a small house with nowhere to go. It was unthinkable.

As if Naomi heard every thought as it suddenly raged through Georgie, she said:

"Remember, you can't look after people the way you used to. They have to look after you. And I don't even mean looking after them physically. I mean, worrying about them. Worry and stress in your condition can set you right back. Right back."

Georgie received every word with a degree of piety.

"Where's that bloody jelly?" said Naomi. "Hang on. But I'll be right back to make you walk a bit. OK?"

Georgie waited, as obedient as a labrador. For the first time in her life she was capitulating and letting herself be organised. If Naomi said she mustn't be stressed, then that was her life-plan from here on.

*

Sam was wonderfully brisk and business-like about her return home.

"I've cleared out the loft room and made it nice for you. Fresh bed linen and everything. You'll need a bed to yourself. I mustn't disturb you. But I won't be far away. You've got a bedside table there with a lamp and I've got some new books ready. Oh and I've ordered one of those stainless steel flasks that keeps liquid cold. I've set the telly up as well. On a table. At the foot of the bed."

Aww, she thought.

"I don't need a telly."

"Ah well. It's there."

She thanked him.

"Oh God, did I tell you? Benjamin's got a job at Sainsbury's. Just to tide him over. They're crying out for staff."

"Is that safe?"

"Oh he'll be fine."

"Are you at each other's throats?"

"Not at all. Happy man cave."

"Won't bother coming home then."

A pause. Led by him.

"I think, on balance, if pushed, I'd rather you did come home."

Another pause. Hers this time.

"Oh go on then."

After the call, she felt a little desolate and waited for the sadness to go away. All around her people slept and panted and coughed, shifted now and again. There had been no attempt by any of them to get to know each other. She had a sense of a degree of shame, in her and the others, because of being there, of having been so weak as to fall foul of a virus, and then by not even being able to control it and send it packing. There was a quiet awe among the medical staff too, which surprised her. Everybody seemed to have been caught short and nobody, neither patient nor nurse, wanted to admit to this level of inexperience.

Why hadn't she asked him about Cherry? Why didn't he tell her? She turned her head and looked at her phone on the bedside table. Sam must be looking after her. He must be taking her food. She didn't understand how the outside world worked but everyone must be looking after everyone else.

*

When Naomi was in, they would talk about the same scripted banalities of diet, exercise and mental well-being before allowing themselves to be a little more honest or adventurous. Naomi was living in quarantine in a hotel for the time being, her family home being out of bounds. She confided more than once that the arrangement suited her down to the ground. She didn't even miss her boyfriend, she laughed. He'd probably rather isolate with her parents than her anyway.

"Everyone has to live in their bubble now," she explained.

Georgie pictured her mother looking forlornly at her through a viscose membrane.

Naomi said her sister, Patricia, had gone to live with her parents, making up their bubble, the three of them having to readjust to a new-old way of living.

"Oh she's lovely, my gorgeous sis," she said, always going into a fond daze as she spoke of her. "She's the really good one in the family. So simple and kind. Not into clothes or anything like that. She's the one who should be in nursing. Though it's not right for her. She needs a family. Kids. Spread the love that way."

"Younger or older than you?" Georgie had asked.

"Older but you wouldn't think it. Much prettier than me. She got the pretty genes. All soft and feminine. Proper chatterbox. Love her."

"But you're helpful, too."

"Not like her. She's kind of accidentally wise, if you know what I mean. She's the type you need beside you. Always a big smile on her face. It's only recently occurred to me, how much we need people who smile a lot and make us feel good about things. They're like medicine."

"I like her name," said Georgie. "I like those names that seem to have taken years to arrive at. Complicated, Anglicised, a bit formal."

Georgie would let herself marvel at Naomi's otherwise unremarkable stories. And she would save her own news for Naomi alone.

"Sam has set up a kind of hospital ward for me at home."

"Aww."

"I've got my own telly and everything."

"Remember not to lie on your back too long, won't you? Your lungs won't like it. And do your breathing exercises."

"Don't worry. I'll never lie on my back again!"

Naomi indicated that Georgie should sit on the side of her bed.

"Are you all right, Georgina? I mean, about going home. Does anything worry you?"

Georgie was a little taken aback. Had she appeared worried?

"No," she said. "Nothing."

"Because you've been through enough anxiety, don't you think?"

Georgie nodded.

"You have to put yourself first from now on. You're very, very weak still. Have you got anyone you can rely on?"

Georgie thought of the sister, of the smiling Patricia, of how Naomi had described a human as medication. There were no such people, she thought. Everyone needed something from you, took a little bit of yourself away with him or her. Nobody gave wholly, not even a loving parent.

"Just sit up and take things slowly and do a little more exercise each day. Take each day at a time."

All the usual platitudes. They meant less and less each time. What could this tiny girl know of the complex interdependencies that existed at Georgie's age – the perpetual cycle of guilt and self-recrimination? Better not even go there. The very thought of it was too exhausting. And so they carried on about the virus, both by now as confidently expert on this mutation as any government medical adviser could ever hope to be.

*

Whenever they were in the room put aside for physiotherapy sessions, Georgie was always surprised to see a sky and some weather outside. She would linger at the window and look out at the silent city, only ambulances passing in and out, silent too. She could tell it was hot – as May often was – and felt sorry for herself and others who had no chance of feeling the sun on their skin. It began to dawn on her that she would like to spend the rest of her life growing flowers. Year after year could be taken up with it, from digging and preparing in the winter, to sowing, nurturing, staking, dead-heading, pruning, cutting back, dividing, and whatever one did to them in the autumn. She would take cuttings so that she could perpetuate their lives and she would do it all alone. No one would be allowed to bother her or intrude on her work.

Wait! Cherry! She had to tell her mother about the flowers. Perhaps they could both do it as a living. Cherry was wonderful at digging gardens. She knew all about it. Yes, that's what they would do together. She must phone her and tell her. That's how she'd break this silence – with the garden plan.

But going home meant having to go outside the hospital and breathing the hazardous air. In the world outside there were roads to cross and items to pay for in shops and conversations to keep going and the news to watch. All of it so complicated. All of it with laws that she'd forgotten. Obligations beyond her.

In the physio room she had her fill of traffic and pedestrians. It was an approximation of society and it would do for her. There were times when she felt a fool, walking perfectly well unaided and performing the rituals they had instilled in her. At others, she wanted to stay the fool, to stumble, perhaps, and to win their concern. Once that level of attention from others had filled her with abhorrence. Now she could barely breathe without seeking permission first.

*

"So, you're sure you'll be looked after properly," said Naomi as they walked slowly back to the ward.

"Oh yes," said Georgie, not even registering the question.

"What's your boy like?"

Georgie was so surprised to get a proper question that she struggled for moment in forming a response.

"He's very beautiful," she said.

"Aww," said Naomi.

"He's at university. Final year."

"Law? Like his mum?"

"No, no," said Georgie, very vague. What was he doing again? Was it history? Maybe politics. Yes, yes, something like that.

"Nothing very useful, I'm afraid," she said.

Naomi didn't seem to be interested any more. She was looking at her phone, her thumb tapping out a message at top speed. "Aww," she said again.

When Naomi looked up, you could tell she was having to recall what had been said. They were moving slowly along the corridor and there were a few moments still left to kill.

"Have you called her yet?" she asked.

Georgie, who had been panting, increased its volume.

I'm scared, she wanted to cry out. *I don't know what state she'll be in. Look after me. Guide me.*

They arrived at Georgie's bed and Naomi watched her charge climb into it.

"Do it now. She'll want to hear your voice. Know you're OK."

Although Georgie was breathing noisily and doing her best to appear incapacitated, Naomi seemed unperturbed and left her to see to other people and hear other confidences.

Georgie reached for her phone and, with effort, calmed herself.

*

"Georgie? Is that you? I'm a little dismayed, to be honest. I'm getting fatter you see. It's not so much the lack of exercise, it's all the food. I've never been a meals person, have I? Little and often. I loved to cook for other people but not for myself. Those lasagnes. Remember those? They were too rich for me. Now I'm getting meals round the clock."

"Who's bringing them, Mum? Is it Sam? Or other people?"

"Bringing them?"

"The meals. The food."

"No, darling. Nobody brings food. He makes the most wonderful meals, you see. Quite irresistible. And I have to be there, parked at the table, or he gets a little cross. He won't mind my saying that. But I could do with some exercise. Are you there now?"

"Am I where?"

"At the park? Shall I come out and join you? I could really do with some fresh air. Are you waiting?"

"You can't go out, Mum. You're not allowed. It's too dangerous."

"Oh I'm not in any danger. Except for not fitting into my clothes. What? I'm only joking. He doesn't mind my saying these things. Not really. So, today's not a walking day? I forget."

No, today's not a walking day.

"I'd better go. Getting looks. Love you, love you."

"Mum! Mum? Same, same."

*

It was excruciating how they clapped her as she left the ward. She'd heard it many times before, the applause as the "survivors" decamped. As if they'd done something clever or entertaining, rather than doggedly held on to life and got lucky. Now it was her turn and she felt trapped in that wheelchair, small and deeply embarrassed.

Before she'd left there had been a forced, rather routine sense of jollity around her among the hospital staff. "Uh oh, who's going to eat all the jelly now?" was the general theme of the banter. "Try not to lie too long on your back," was the measured advice.

She would press her lips together and deliver a smile in response to everything.

She said "I'll never be able to thank you enough" a hundred times.

"Aww," they all replied.

Naomi was off that day and they hadn't had the wit to say their goodbyes days before. Anyway, the decision to discharge her had come very quickly. Georgie asked everyone to give Naomi her love, to thank her properly and with meaning. Without that young woman she would have been crushed by the hospital experience. She had been looked after in such an efficient and down-to-earth way that she'd been able to sink gratefully into the care of another, with no sense of awkwardness. One day she would show her gratitude properly and not by proxy as she was forced to now. It unsettled her, this lack of leave-taking. She fixed Naomi in her mind, didn't want to let go of her.

A male doctor was standing by the side, laughing with two nurses. She looked up at him from the wheelchair and recognised him. The badge said Benjamin. She hadn't seen him since she'd first come round.

He stooped to speak to her.

"I expect you to be much better in the next few weeks," he said.

How could he possibly know?

"But sometimes people feel a bit strange, maybe have bad memories of being on the ventilator. Panic even."

"I don't remember anything about it," she told him.

"Yes, fortunately you weren't on there too long. All the same, it can haunt you a bit, being attached to that machine."

"I'll be fine," she said. "I'll have my family to distract me."

"Great."

"My husband's bought in a tonne of jelly." She felt stupid as soon as she'd said it. It had worked on the nurses. Dr Efren Benjamin was non-plussed.

"What would I do anyway?" she asked. "I mean, if I felt funny about it?"

"A good question," he reflected. "This is all a bit new to all of us."

I used to appreciate honesty, she thought. *Not any more.*

A porter took hold of the wheelchair handles and they began their applauded journey down the corridor. Then it was just the two of them in the lift. And finally the air and the outside. Georgie stood up and stepped away from the wheelchair and closed her eyes because the sun was so strong. The end of May. Two months of her life gone, spent in the building behind her, caught and held, and now released.

"Mum!"

She opened her eyes to see her husband and her son, in t-shirts, shorts and with masks over the lower halves of their faces. Their eyes were wide at the sight of her. It occurred to her that she probably looked utterly ravaged and nothing like the woman they had last seen being taken away by an ambulance. But she couldn't care less.

10

Under the skylight the world reduced itself to her and it. Clouds slid past and, propped up on three large (new) pillows, she watched them arrive and disappear beyond the window frame. Far above her, the empty, silent sky. Far below, the people who clattered pans and slammed doors.

   In the loft bedroom, made clean and comfortable by her husband, Georgie sat in bed and, whatever position she moved into, her eyes always sought the skylight and the clouds. She had never known a lightness like it; an emptiness. That week falsely asleep, the machine keeping her lungs working, had somehow devitalised her, taken away a little bit of blood, bone, breath and flesh. It wasn't so much exhaustion, as cluelessness. Things happened – she was fed, visited, checked – but she had no idea what she was meant to do about it. Was she supposed to change? Was there another her that they were waiting to have restored to them? Perhaps she should explain that that wasn't going to happen, that something had gone and that she was a remnant now. She could attempt to explain but the right language eluded her. In the hospital she had responded very happily to questions but in the hospital they understood what had happened to her. There was no need for any explanation. They knew her blood count, her oxygen level, her muscle mass, the exact amount of salt and iron in her system. They knew all these things without having to ask. They knew her better than she did herself. Outside the hospital, she would have to describe how she felt and that was almost impossible. She wouldn't be able to elucidate on what that moment was like when they said she might not wake up or the searing shock of actually waking up. The pain in her throat, the looseness of her limbs. None of it came across at all impressively when put into words. Best not to try. And so Georgie decided that, when it came to the administrations of Sam and Benjamin, she would accept it all quietly and keep her thoughts to herself. They wanted to look after her but they also had their lives to lead and didn't need to know about her dark dreams and the way her voice sounded so different in her head. On her first evening home, the sky pale but lustrous at teatime, she decided she wouldn't say a word to anyone about anything. Ever.

*

A young woman was standing at the door. Georgie had opened her eyes, faintly hungry, and been surprised to see a stranger in the doorway. The girl was smiling broadly at her, though her expression was a complicated business, radiating friendliness, concern, fear, shyness, confusion, serenity and gentleness – all making their way across her face like the clouds through the skylight.

"Can I get you anything?" the young woman asked. "Are you comfortable? Have you got everything you need?"

Georgie narrowed her eyes and examined her visitor. She had just woken up from a dream where she was packing the contents of the bathroom cabinet into a suitcase and explaining to Sam that they needed to sell everything, only the things in the cabinet shouldn't have been there, being largely pens, knitting needles and crucifixes. The line between dream and consciousness was so blurred these days. You couldn't be sure you were fully awake half the time.

"Anything at all?" the girl asked.

"No," said Georgie. "Thank you."

The young woman was in jeans and tan leather sandals. She wore a white T-shirt and you could see the abundance of her breasts through the fabric. Her skin was smooth and warm in colour. Her hair was thick with brown waves, worn short and shaggy.

"Who are you?" asked Georgie.

The girl's eyes widened and her hand shot up to her mouth to stifle the sound of her laughter. Georgie shuddered, astonished.

"I'm Beatrice," said the visitor.

But who are you? Why are you here? I won't talk to anyone. About anything.

The girl advanced hesitatingly into the room. When she was close enough to touch Georgie, she stopped. The smell of cut grass reached Georgie's nostrils. From the open window or from the girl? It made her eyes fill.

"Have you been outside?"

"You have such a lovely garden," said Beatrice. "I've been helping to keep it tidy. I hope you don't mind." She frowned before delivering another broad smile. "Oh my God! They didn't tell you. I'm here because I'm part of your bubble. You know, isolating with you."

"Benjamin," said Georgie, trying to follow.

"That's right. I'm with him. I didn't want to quarantine alone and so I'm here. It's very kind of you all to have me. I really want to make sure I do my bit. I'd love to help you get better, if that's not weirding you out or anything. Or just keep you company. Would that be OK? Anything, anything at all that you want. Oh and I totally get that the last thing you fancy is reliving what must have happened to you. I want to know – don't get me wrong – but I've thought about it and I think if I were in your shoes I wouldn't really want to go back and explain it all. I'd want to be on factory reset. Do you know what I mean? Oh my God, I talk so much, don't I? It's nerves. I mean, I so admire you, your job and everything, and I hope to get to know you. It's weird now, isn't it? Me, talking."

Georgie's eyelids were fluttering closed. The past half minute, listening to this strange juddering monologue, had instantly taken her back to the disjointed babble of the hospital ward and so soothed her that she could barely stay awake.

"Beatrice," she said.

"Yes?" came the girl's voice. "Really, anything at all. At your service. Something to eat?"

Georgie was aware of returning a smile.

"Come back in the morning to see me."

*

Doors slamming. Feet on the stairs. Voices. The phone ringing. Birds.

And now the television, too. Sam had switched it on for her, insisting that they watch something together. He sat beside her on the bed. It was the news – endless stories about people suffocating to death. To escape it, she looked inside the TV and admired its wires and circuit boards, followed a beautifully intermeshed pattern of leads and cables.

"I'm sorry," said Sam. He'd been holding her hand and now squeezed it to signal his apology. "I didn't think. This must be awful for you."

He waited. He wanted to know. She was fully aware of that. He must have felt that this was the moment for her to tell him what had happened. *I remember*, she'd have to say. *It was just the same for me, the gasping for air.*

But no, she wouldn't, and when Benjamin came up to see them after his shift at the supermarket, Sam seemed relieved.

"Some dinner?" he asked.

"Yes, please. I'm shattered and starving."

Georgie glanced shyly at her son. She felt unable to claim him, he was so different to her memory of the boy-man she had seen head back to university half a year before. When he was young – right up to his mid-teens – Benjamin had been hers and Cherry's. The three of them had been so close that they talked a common language based on the games they played, the children's TV programmes they watched and the toys that were in favour. And then Benjamin had simply rejected them, gone looking for his father and a man's world. He grew to match Sam in height and if he was out with his parents, he would always walk with Sam, not her, like he was cleaving to a close friend. It didn't bother her in the slightest. She talked about it often with Cherry, not with any sense of regret but only of wonder.

Whose idea, she pondered, was it to bring Benjamin's girlfriend on board? To allow her to ruin the perfect pairing? Was Beatrice so panicked at being without her boyfriend that she somehow insinuated her way into their home? Was it just that Benjamin couldn't live without sex? Maybe Cherry was right – that the young male needed sex on call to keep him contented. Was that the girl's purpose? Even in that short meeting earlier, Georgie had worked out that Benjamin would have been the dominant of the two and Beatrice the acquiescing type. The girl was definitely one of life's obligers.

"Are you tired?" Sam asked Georgie.

Georgie said she thought she was.

"Then we'll leave you. Lots of sleep, OK?"

That had been the most she'd said to him all evening. Hand-squeezing had been their sole means of communication. Sam, never garrulous himself, didn't feel uncomfortable in the silence, seemed content simply to sit with her. But now his son was home, there were other duties to perform and he came alive with the prospect of cooking for his boy.

Benjamin leant down but stopped short of kissing Georgie – as if she could catch it again! – but even then she could smell the cardboard and the plastic packaging.

"Love you, Mum."

Sam pulled the door half closed as he and Benjamin made their way downstairs. She liked it fully open but wasn't going to call after them. She could hear their uneven footsteps as they jostled for space on the narrow loft staircase. Georgie sank down under the duvet, pulled her legs up to her chest, felt her bony kneecaps in her palm.

The men's voices were still wafting up and reaching her, despite their lowered tones and the half-shut door.

"Shall we tell her about Gran?" asked Benjamin. "About the food being rejected. About that guy."

His father shushed him.

"Not now. When she's stronger. It's not going to change anytime soon, anyway."

Their footsteps died away as they retreated from her world.

11

"Are you allowed out?" Georgie asked the girl.

Beatrice was sitting on the edge of the bed. It was mid-morning and she was back in the loft bedroom, obligingly, as she had been asked.

"Oh yes, definitely. We're allowed half an hour of exercise every day. That can mean going for a run or walking the dog or just plain walking, actually."

"Half an hour is enough," said Georgie, relaxing back into her pillows.

"Oh and shopping. We can go out to get food for ourselves or for others. It's very weird, isn't it. Benjamin says there are fights in Sainsbury's over toilet paper. You're better off out of it."

"There's so much noise in the world," said Georgie, distractedly. She was staring at the blank TV screen. "People telling you what you should do and eat and how you should look and talk. I wonder why we put up with it."

Beatrice wriggled on the mattress, as though she were screwing her buttocks in place.

"You're not talking about lockdown now, are you?"

"Just life in general," said Georgie. "I felt it most when I had a new baby. Information coming at me from everywhere. There doesn't seem to be a single over-riding line on anything. Everyone thinks they know best based on their own narrow lives."

"When I have a baby, I'll just do everything by instinct."

Georgie turned her eyes to Beatrice. "I think that's a very good idea. Block out all the noise."

The girl was basking in Georgie's approval.

"Not that I'm planning on anything like that for a long time."

"What are you studying at university?" asked Georgie.

"It's not very interesting. Honestly."

Beatrice was in the same T-shirt and jeans that morning. She said she had breakfasted in the garden with the others, "on that really cool patio thing".

"The terrace," said Georgie.

About now the tulips would have faded and the forget-me-nots and nigella would be spreading their delicate latticework across the beds. As though Beatrice was following her thoughts, she asked: "Shall I bring you in some flowers? To put by your bedside."

Georgie was about to say yes, but then changed her mind. "No thank you," she said. "I'd rather see them in situ."

"You mean you're coming down?"

"No. I'm nowhere near strong enough. I went to the top of the stairs last night and couldn't get much further."

Beatrice looked at the back of her hands. Georgie let her eyes rest on them as well, saw clear, smooth skin and strong, ringless fingers.

"Benjamin says you're not talking much," said Beatrice quietly, as though she was broaching something painful. Georgie didn't feel any pain at all.

"I'm not. Except to you. Funny, isn't it?"

"Maybe because I'm neutral, that kind of thing."

"Maybe."

More absorption in the hand by both women.

Then suddenly, finally, Georgie got down to it.

"Would you mind – if you haven't done your daily half hour – directing your walk to the estate down the hill? All I ask is that you go past my mother's house and see if everything is all right."

Now Beatrice seemed uncomfortable, squirming on the bed, her sunny expression clouding over.

"I…I'm not sure. We're not supposed to see other people, are we? I mean, we don't even know how easy it is to pass it on to others. Just touching something, spreading it…that could be really dangerous. And she's frail, isn't she?"

Frail? Cherry Weston frail? Were they talking about the same woman?

"What have they told you?" Georgie wanted to know.

"About your mum? Nothing."

"Have they talked about her?"

"All I know is that Benjamin's dad, I mean Sam, tried to take some food to her a couple of times but brought it back."

Georgie sat up straight.

"Why?"

"Because that man told them it wasn't needed."

"*That man?*"

"We don't know his name."

"The Youngster," said Georgie faintly.

Beatrice leant in closer to Georgie, mildly panicked. "I haven't told you anything you don't already know, right?"

It was true. She hadn't.

"My mother isn't remotely frail. Not physically anyway. She smashed up a patio almost single-handed."

"Gosh. Why?"

"Why what?"

"What made her want to smash up a patio?"

She wasn't going to send this girl to spy on Cherry. It wasn't fair on her. But maybe if she knew what to look for then she might one day spot Cherry on one of her walks. Or maybe even befriend her. They could walk together. Through her, Georgie and Cherry could return to each other.

"To make a beautiful new home for herself. You'd like it. Her little house. Red front door. I'll tell you where it is."

*

Sometimes her dreams were delightful, dark corners of a garden where her mind rested gratefully, old, tall houses where she could roam undisturbed, a market of flowers and meandering animals. Sometimes they shocked her awake: Sam and Cherry looking on unmoved as she pulled an oily chain out of her throat, link after dripping link, unable to tell them how scared she was, hoping they would notice, watching them walk away. It was the lottery of her sleep-filled days. Sam was convinced that it was doing her good, all that sleep. Perhaps it was, bodily speaking. But increasingly it gave her a sense of her own decomposition.

"You have nothing to worry about anymore, Geeny," said Sam one evening a week after her return. He was placing a glass of lemon barley water on the bedside table along with a buttered hot cross bun. "All you need to do is eat and sleep. That's all. Nothing else matters."

But her face suggested otherwise. He sat down on the side of her bed and watched her for a while, his hand searching for hers.

"Is it work? Don't worry about that. You're on indefinite leave. They often ask after you."

She gripped on to his hand when it arrived and shook her head. Sam sighed deeply.

"It's your mum, isn't it? Listen, I know it's a hard thing to do but try and put her out of your mind. She's doing really well. She's got some friend staying with her who's looking after her. He's in the spare room and doing all her shopping and cleaning and everything. The thing is she's got companionship which lots of older people haven't right now. When this is all over, you'll be back to your walks. I met him, actually, when I took some food round. Had a chat. He's clearly fussing over her and utterly devoted. That's good, isn't it?"

Who was Sam trying to convince? It sounded like himself. Georgie cleared her throat. She couldn't stay silent for ever.

"Did you see her? Was she there?"

Sam looked around the room as though he were taking a quick impromptu inventory.

"You've got nothing to worry about." He was squeezing her fingers so hard that she tightened her jaw to endure it. "Just sleep and eat. Concentrate on that."

*

On the fifth attempt she finally got through. By then she was imagining all kinds of horrors. It was eleven at night.

"Georgie girl?"

"Mum!"

"Can't you sleep either?"

"No, Mama, I can't."

"My mind is racing."

Georgie couldn't quite believe that she was talking to Cherry at last. It felt like they were glimpsing each other from passing boats. Their time was limited.

"Mama, I never tell you how much I love you."

"Georgie! You don't need to. I know it."

"Do you? You know that sometimes I don't call because I don't have the energy. Not because I don't want to."

It felt like they didn't have long, like the boats were moving away at speed. Her mother's mind seemed so clear and as of old. Maybe she was having a good day.

"I was remembering," said Cherry, "that we once fell out, years ago, because I'd bought you a pet rabbit and you didn't want it and said you couldn't look after it properly and that we didn't have space for it. I thought it was so funny because usually it's the children who want the pets and the parents say no."

"I'm so sorry that we fell out over that."

"Oh, not at all. I'm sorry. I'm sorry, Georgie, that I sometimes didn't get you. Did it spoil your childhood?"

Georgie gasped.

"Spoil it? Why on earth are you asking that? I had the happiest childhood."

"You did?"

"You know I did."

"Yes, I thought so. Then you're not angry about the rabbit?"

"Oh Mum."

She had so much to say, wanted to discuss a raft of childhood memories. How funny that they were both in the same mood. How typical of them to be in tune.

"And then there was – "

But her mother stopped, or *was* stopped, her voice disappearing. Georgie heard a male voice say "nope" and the line went dead. For a moment, she waited open-mouthed, a blank, not understanding or knowing anything. Then she called again, and again, and again. Nothing each time. She was helpless. Was that the source of her pain? That someone else was helping her mother and not her? She only wanted to speak to her, to reminisce, to aid her recovery by smiling her way through forgotten stories. The rabbit. Did that really happen? She couldn't remember it. She'd always longed for a pet – why had she turned this potential new companion down? Might it be because she was a hard-hearted little know-it-all as a child, conversant with emotional manipulation at such an early age? Was that the real Georgie?

Or maybe it never happened.

She called her mother's phone once more and then screamed silently – the rage all inside – when, as she fully expected, nobody answered.

*

It seemed to Georgie that there might only be two people on the planet at that moment unconcerned about the pandemic: her and Beatrice. They talked – usually in the mornings – about all manner of arbitrary topics but never about illness or case numbers. For Georgie the subject was over and to let herself dwell on it meant failing to recover. For Beatrice, miraculously, it simply didn't feature at all in her daily thinking. The girl was good-natured to the point of two-dimensionality. She either asked after Georgie in detail or twittered happily about Benjamin and how extraordinarily clever and handsome he was. Which, to a large extent, Georgie agreed with – although she worried that the young woman might be fawning over him a little too much.

She met him, Beatrice said, when she went to see him playing in his band at college.

"Did you know about his band? It's called Prod."

"Yes, I know all about Prod," said Georgie. "I heard every detail about its birth. I assumed it was all over."

"It is now. Everything's over now. Benjamin won't even be able to graduate properly."

Georgie thought of her boy stacking supermarket shelves at that very moment.

"He won't mind. He was raring to get out into the world of work. Anyway, he more or less finished his degree in time. That's all that matters."

"I know that!" said Beatrice, hotly. There was nothing about Benjamin she wasn't abreast of. She didn't need to be told.

"Will *you* be all right, about *your* degree, I mean?"

Beatrice, who never talked about her own studies, shrugged.

"Today," said Georgie, "I'm going out into the garden. And then soon I shall go out for my daily exercise. Beatrice, I've never asked, but can you drive?"

The girl seemed startled by the question.

"No, I can't, I'm sorry."

"No problem," said Georgie breezily. "No problem at all. Then we shall walk, that's all. Easy."

"Walk? Where are we walking?"

Georgie was often on the brink of laughing when she talked to her new young friend. It was such an amusing, baiting kind of experience.

"Not far. Just down to the estate. Ten minutes, no more. No need to disturb Sam or Benjamin about it. But I'd love you to come with me, just in case. Is that all right with you?"

Beatrice thought about it, her features betraying the inner dialogue. When it was resolved she seemed bright and happy once again.

"Yeah, let's do it," she said. "Let's go for a little walk. Why not? But it won't be for a while yet. You and I both know that."

She was right. Walking all the way to Cherry's house, as close as it was, was a mountain that Georgie still wasn't quite ready to climb.

12

Doors slamming. Cars starting. Someone practising the piano. Neighbours calling across to each other from a safe distance. A plane passing across the skylight – though rarely these days – cutting through the thick early summer air like an iron along a board.

Georgie slept on in her attic room, turning on one side then the other, reached for her new flask and sipped the cold water. Feet on the narrow wooden steps meant someone was checking on her. Occasionally her visitor would stand at the threshold, not daring to come in and wake her. Benjamin. He seemed almost too scared to approach her, fearful that he might re-infect her from his workmates and the customers. Sam came in with a purpose, to bring her food or to watch the news with her. She lay curled up beside him as he glowered through the press conference where his senior colleague gave his excuses for breaking lockdown rules. Georgie felt his tension and sensed Sam's disapproval. She remembered that particular advisor from Whitehall but had no interest at all in what he had to say.

Sam brought her food and took the plates away. He always stopped to look down at her and she would smile up at him. Better soon.

One morning, he came up to tell her that he was having a remote meeting at midday and lunch would be late. It only occurred to her later that she could relieve Sam of his serving duties by asking Beatrice to take them on. Would he mind? He seemed to like fussing around her but it wasn't fair when work was so demanding to ask him to butter toast or heat up soup. No, that would be better taken care of by the girl. It was the first time that Georgie wondered how Beatrice had fitted into the family before her return from hospital. How did she keep up a conversation with Sam? Had she complicated the very easy relationship between father and son? She couldn't imagine Sam living easily alongside this gauche, self-effacing young woman.

Later, when Beatrice looked in on her, Georgie wanted to make it clear how appreciated she was, just in case Sam had neglected to do so.

"I'll miss you when this is all over and you've gone."

Beatrice was sheepish. "I think everyone is OK with me being here so, if it's all right with you, I'd like to stay a little longer. I think I'm good for you."

Georgie laughed at Beatrice's audacity.

"You are! You're very good for me."

Is this what it's like to have a daughter? To be met in the middle?

"Tomorrow," said Beatrice. "Tomorrow, I'll go to the house and see what I can see."

*

When Georgie woke, she saw Beatrice sitting in the doorway, her back against the doorframe, her knees up to her chin. She was looking at her phone, deeply absorbed. Her hair was hanging over her face and all Georgie could see was the pale tip of a nose. Still in those jeans and a white T-shirt. Maybe she kept it to that simple combination because she knew how good she looked in it and there was no need for any further experimentation. That degree of self-knowledge deeply impressed Georgie who had struggled all her life to find a single satisfactory outfit, no matter how assiduously she studied others who had the knack. She could never dress like Cherry, wasn't built that way anyway, but beyond her mother she never came across well-dressed people. At work it was suits for men, suits for women. A silk scarf was an act of flamboyance, something to be remarked upon. She owned at least ten silk scarves, had worn them very rarely.

"Hello," she said quietly.

Beatrice looked up and Georgie felt warmed through at once. To wake up and see her in the doorway was to feel guarded.

"Nothing," said Beatrice. "I'm ever so sorry."

Georgie didn't understand. Beatrice got up and settled herself, as ever, on the bed.

"I hung around the house and didn't see a thing. The whole street was empty. The whole estate. I went as close as I dared – a few feet away from the door – and waited about a bit, ready to run, but there was no sign of life. Maybe they were in the garden, chilling together, that kind of thing."

The idea of Cherry and the Youngster chilling in the garden instantly darkened Georgie's mood. It was her mother's garden. They had worked on it together. It was for her to enjoy, not some interloper.

"Really? Nothing? No movement at all?"

"No. Sorry. It's a funny place though, isn't it? Not like here. I walked through the estate to get back to the road and some houses were really nice and neat and others were disgusting. How are people managing to stay indoors in such tiny flats and houses? I heard this woman really shouting at her kids – fuck this, fuck that – like a total midwife."

"What?" asked Georgie, a little lost in the exposition. "Oh, you mean fishwife."

"Yeah, fishwife. Whatever one of those is."

He's in the back bedroom. Living there. Cherry hadn't even finished decorating it. He's sleeping in the guest bed. Cherry had bought the bed for her daughter or her grandson, in case it was ever needed. Not for a stranger.

Who else, wondered Georgie, knew Cherry well enough to question the situation? There was a doctor, a GP that they'd visited together, Croft she was called. She was impatiently courteous, distractedly concerned. The first time they had met her, after Cherry had grown worried about her memory, mother and daughter had sat and listened, daughter holding back, waiting for mother, but mother didn't take the lead. When they got outside, Georgie had exploded. "Why didn't you ask questions? It was almost like you didn't want to know."

Cherry had smiled. "Would *you* want to know?"

Always having to scrape together the facts, looking on the internet because Cherry wouldn't. It drove her crazy. Why did she have to do everything for everyone! A beautiful woman, elegantly deteriorating, and with no clue as to how long it would take, no means of planning or preparing but, maddeningly, taking it each day at a time.

And now someone who would make her tea and cook her meals. A friend, a protector. At a time when anxiety was fed to them every day on the news, a virus that came from far away and was seemingly cutting them down, Cherry wasn't alone, needed to fear nothing, because she was looked after.

Georgie picked up her phone and called her mother. As she expected, the phone wasn't answered. She called again. She ended up leaving three messages. In one she even resorted to saying that she was feeling very unwell. Beatrice looked on, tiny frown marks giving away her concern. Downstairs Sam was on the phone, talking to a colleague, a world away.

*

Looking in the mirror was bewildering. For the past few years she had avoided her reflection, depressed by her rapid ageing, but now, gaunt, she was fascinated. Her eyelids were folded over her eyes, like window blinds, her cheeks bookended by incised lines. Her hair – she couldn't remember when she'd last had it dyed – was like an animal pelt: thick, rough and black steaked with white. None of it appalled her. But it wasn't *her*, exactly, this image in the mirror. Or was this the new her? The one she would have to get used to.

Beatrice stood at the doorway of the little en suite shower room and watched as Georgie pushed the skin of her cheeks up to her eyes then let it drop.

"I do that too."

"Not to this extent you don't. Everything is so loose now. Like it isn't my skin at all, like I've got the wrong size on."

"You've just lost a lot of weight, that's all. You'll fill out again, don't worry."

A girl of effortless beauty, unlined, firm all over, what could she possibly know? And yet, how comforting to be told by her that there would be a physical reversal. It wasn't just consoling, it was convincing. Like it was coming from a nurse.

Georgie went back into the bedroom and patted the bed to encourage Beatrice to join her.

"I hope Benjamin is good to you," she said. "I hope he appreciates you."

The pause worried her. All pauses meant trouble.

"I think I get on his nerves a bit."

Georgie had been half-expecting an answer along those lines but was disheartened all the same. The day before, Benjamin had come upstairs before going to work, as he always did, and kissed her goodbye on her head. Usually, she was half asleep but this time she had held out her hand for his.

"I've gotta go, Mum, sorry. I'm late."

"All right, go. But thank you."

"What for?"

He stood looking down at her, as tall– no, taller than his father, the same fine brown hair and small nose, the same squarish jaw. The same jittery impatience with anything personal.

"For letting me share your lovely girl."

His expression was rigid, his mouth half open. He seemed to be shrinking away from her. It felt like he wanted to talk to her but didn't have the words. She should have known. Now they'd both think she was interfering and resent her.

"Beatrice is very special. I'm grateful, that's all."

Which only made it worse because he cut her off. "Mum. Why are we talking about her now?"

"Go to work," she'd said. "I won't say another word."

And now here was the proof that things were not well, his unease mirrored in his girlfriend's cringing expression. Oh the complicated, masochistic nature of young relationships. She didn't miss any of it.

Beatrice was settling on the bed beside her, doing that screwing-down action of hers, fixing herself in place.

"Is he short-tempered with you?" Georgie asked. "He can be a bit fiery, my boy. Sorry. Maybe his father was the same at his age. They grow out of it. I shouldn't really interfere, but I can say something if it'll help."

"No!"

Georgie was surprised by such vehemence.

"Please don't say anything," begged Beatrice. "Don't talk about me at all. I like just being here. I know it sounds funny, but I've always preferred being on the edge of everything. I don't like being in the centre, people looking in at me."

"I suppose you see and hear things better that way," agreed Georgie. "But are you sure?"

"I'm quite sure. It makes me feel ill to think I'm being talked about."

"You're a funny thing."

"I thought you might feel the same way."

Georgie gave it some thought. Not for the first time, the girl had found a hidden latch, opened a forgotten door. Usually, it made Georgie want to end the conversation. Not today.

"I don't know what I really am, to be honest," said Georgie. "I've become something, something assertive, cold and clipped, but I don't think that's really me."

"You're not cold. Not in the slightest. Who says you are?"

"I sometimes think it. I can be rather forbidding at work. I know full well."

"Maybe there's something inside you that's telling you how to behave in a particular situation. And it's telling you that at work you don't need to be friendly, you need to work. You're not cold with your family."

"Sometimes I am."

"No. I've seen you. And I've seen you with them. You're just not particularly demonstrative, none of you."

Now they were getting to the core of it.

"Are we strange and unusual? Is that what you're saying?"

"Of course not," exclaimed Beatrice, horrified. "You're perfect as you are. Honest. I can tell Sam worships you."

"Oh come on!"

"He *does*. You're his goddess."

They were laughing now. Beatrice was lying back on the pillow beside Georgie, who was shushing her. She didn't want Sam to hear them, not least because she still barely spoke to him, and it would be a kick in the teeth to hear her prattling away in the loft with their guest.

"Hang on," said Beatrice, controlling herself. "Can you hear that? Is it your phone?"

Georgie scrambled to find the phone under her duvet.

"It's my mum," she said, elated. "Thank God."

Beatrice sat up, moved down to the foot of the bed, as ever wriggling away from the centre of the action. Georgie grinned at her, waggled her head in victory. She answered the call.

"Mum?"

"Georgie?"

"Mama, oh thank goodness. It's impossible to get hold of you these days."

"It's a bit confusing if…"

She was stopped. Georgie heard, once again, the "nope".

For a moment the universe waited, hanging on her next move. A second, no more, but it was excruciating.

"Stop! Don't put the phone down on me. Who is this, please?"

Another gap, another long-seeming wait. But at least the phone wasn't being switched off.

"Who is this? Speak to me or put my mother back on."

Then his voice, arriving out of the silence, new to her ear, peculiar, wrong. So, here he was at last. The Youngster.

13

He said: "Cheryl is a little confused at the moment."

He said it with authority and forbearance. There was a faint regional accent, a rather prissy one, and it was delivered at a slightly feminine pitch. He seemed to have nothing more to say.

"What do you mean?" she asked. "How do you mean confused?"

In that second, she felt hate. Like a sting from nowhere. The venom was coursing through her and entering every organ. He was claiming her mother for himself already, taking her name, using his own version. She heard him sigh, which enraged her. She looked across at Beatrice, frowning fiercely at her. Was he for real? How dare he?

"There are days," he said, picking through his words like he was doing it with his fingertips, "where she finds it difficult to work out what's going on. On those days I don't think it's a good idea that she uses the phone. It upsets her. I am only trying to look after her and do what's best for her. She loves her exercise and that's all well and good but for the time being it's best for her not to be stimulated."

Georgie was struggling to form the right words, stumbling over his sentences, trying to grasp what he was saying, affronted that she should have to do so.

"I'm sorry," she said. "Who *are* you?"

Another little tut, another sad sigh.

"I'm only trying to look after her. Otherwise, she'd be alone."

"She isn't alone. My husband and son have been looking in on her. I was ill."

"Ah well. You all took your eye off the ball, then. It happens. Strange times."

Was he castigating her or consoling her? And who was he to do either?

"I've been worried about her. I need to know that I can talk to her. Every day."

"I'm sorry," he said. "I don't think that's a good idea. I'll give her the phone when I think she'll be up to using it. I'm trying to make her happy, you see."

The call ended. He'd ended it, not Georgie. She spoke into the deadness, asking if he was there. She dialled back. The phone wasn't answered.

When she looked at Beatrice's face, she saw her own consternation and horror looking back at her.

"What the fuck?" she said. "What just happened?"

Beatrice seemed stunned. Had she heard? Was she just working from Georgie's answers? She leaned across the bed, got Georgie in her sights.

"You need to find the strength to sort this out," she said, and not for the first time this barely-formed child of a woman was cutting through the noise and confusion and setting Georgie on the right track. Yes, she needed all her strength to deal with the confrontation that was coming. Her line of communication with her mother was down but she would meet this catastrophe head on, would go to the little house on the estate and turf this self-satisfied bastard out once and for all.

*

She slept, remembering, her dreams imprinted with moments from a long swathe of the past. Cherry in her boutique, Georgie in the corner, nestled in the stock room, waiting for her mother to close up and take them home. Cherry releasing Benjamin as Georgie came home from work, letting mother and son collide happily, looking on. Cherry at the doctor's surgery, tamping down questions, keeping herself together for the sake of her daughter. Cherry waiting in her house for Georgie to come and visit, not at all clear why she wasn't there. Were they even dreams or were they accusations?

*

When she'd applied for a job in the Office of the Parliamentary Counsel she was interviewed by its head, Angus Gilmartin, now *Sir* Angus Gilmartin, and he'd seemed almost casually shrewd to her, a hobbyist reader of people.

"You've been doing case law for two departments. Why step across? This is a very different discipline," he said.

Georgie had prepared several impressive answers to take on every possible question. But now it came to it, she could only express the purity of her feelings.

"I want to climb right inside it. *Be* it."

He watched her a moment, thinking, before responding.

"When people are asked about the most important jobs in society they usually answer doctor, nurse, police officer, that kind of thing. But without *us*, there wouldn't even be a society. They have no idea."

"And that's as it should be," she said, to which he smiled.

No one need know how important they were. It was just a job, an un-jumbling and laying flat, a service that kept official life ticking. Oh there was nothing more beautiful – was there? – than trammelling life and keeping it there where it could be tinkered with from time to time but always kept in order. From where they were, the makers of law, they could see it all laid flat before them and amend as they went along. It was exhilarating. It was her perfect home.

*

She would need Sam. Finally, she would have to talk to him about how she felt and what she had been through. With that understanding between them, that clarity, he would drop everything else and see to this most pressing need: the extrication of the Youngster. Sam was not a physical or hot-headed kind of person but there were times when he could be quite definitive about things. He'd acquired a toughened skin in the Cabinet Office, defending himself from the ready blame that his political masters threw at him when things went wrong. Sam would listen and then he would question her, but he would understand and want to sort it all out.

Beatrice backed out of the room whenever Sam entered with the tray.

"You should come down to dinner now and eat with us," he said the evening of the call with the Youngster. "Maybe this could be your last dinner in bed. Do you want the telly on?"

Georgie pushed herself up into sitting position and accepted the tray on her lap.

She had a lot to say to him, had rehearsed all her instructions, but instead she shook her head to decline the TV offer.

He pulled up a chair and sat beside her while she ate, telling her about how much he was enjoying working remotely and not having to go into the office although, now she was stronger and seeing as he was classed as a key worker, he would probably venture into Whitehall soon.

"Will you be all right?" he asked. "Being here alone."

Not for the first time it occurred to her that father and son might not be the perfect hosts for poor Beatrice, never seeming to spend much time with her, not caring what she was up to or whether she was content to be knocking about the house while they were busy. Neither Sam nor Benjamin appeared to have changed their ways to allow for the needs of their guest. No wonder she and Beatrice had found each other, given the girl's evident isolation. But then what would a busy, middle-aged professional male have to say to a naïve young woman who had attached herself to his family? Georgie wondered what dinner time was like, the three of them making conversation about their day, none of them with anything remotely interesting to impart, probably talking about *her*, and picking apart her condition and waiting for her to come and break up the dull trio and inject some novel notes. Did Beatrice contribute anything at all? Or was she too nervous about being laughed at and dismissed? What an oddly insecure creature Benjamin had found for himself. But then the girl was so lovely and so good-natured and affectionate that you could see why anyone would want to keep her to himself.

Sam looked on and when she'd finished her food, he removed the tray and placed it on the floor. He leant in and picked up her right hand, anchoring it fast in both of his.

This was the moment, then, for her to be honest, to tell him about her nightmares, about the chain dragging through her throat, and all the other shocking images that assailed her semi-conscious brain. And her anger and hate. He needed to know about the pounding animosity she felt for the interloper and how urgently he had to be got rid of.

Sam's hands tightened around hers. How strange...*he* wanted to talk. He already had his agenda items set out. He was beating her to it.

"So, Geeny, we've been through a lot in the last couple of months and I know this sounds insane but I'm rather satisfied with life at the moment. You're doing well. I'm at home and can keep an eye on you and know that you're safe. Benjamin comes and goes and I prize my evening chats with him. We're all together. It's rather precious. It makes me think that we'll both enjoy our retirement."

She couldn't speak but listened instead, kept her eyes on his face, watched his lips.

"It's what they say about a nest, isn't it? All of us safe at home together. The world's gone mad out there but we're at home. I know it's terribly difficult for a lot of people, but I can't help finding some pleasure in it. Would you agree?"

Georgie nodded her agreement.

"It's not quite normal, any of it, and yet there's such a rightness to it. Maybe our lives are being stripped down to all that matters. You're better and you're here and we're all together."

He shook his head in wonder.

"So good to be together."

But we're not all here together. One of us is missing. She should be here, protected, fed and looked after by us. She's with a stranger. Don't you care? Have you forgotten?

No, her husband would not be the one to deal robustly with this man. Not Sam. He didn't like the boat rocked at the best of times, used to be a little bored by the thought of having to entertain his mother-in-law even when things were right with her brain. He had always been accepting of her, particularly when she had made things so harmonious with a new baby in the house, but there wasn't a real fondness there. When Cherry was diagnosed, he had suggested to Georgie that her mother might need to be in a home, sooner rather than later, for fear that the bulk of her care would land with her daughter. Or even him. "It's not going to be easy," he'd counselled the indignant Georgie who couldn't bring herself to look at him for days after he'd brought up the issue of a care home.

Not Sam, then. It would have to be her son. Benjamin would be the brute force, the authority, the strength she needed when she didn't have enough of her own. Sam could go and fuss over his papers at his desk. Benjamin was out in the real world. He'd bring Cherry home.

14

When he was small, he held her hand all the time, particularly when they were out and the environment seemed a little dangerous without that linked chain between mother and son. She'd feel it arrive, the small palm, fingers curling round hers, and then she knew that he was happy and secure. He worried, when young, thought the world beyond their street was full of unpredictability and danger, unfamiliar people, erratic, capricious children. His father's son, then; wary of those who weren't quite like him. He would stay silent on their walk to the park, concentrate on both of them getting there without mishap. Once there, usually with both mother and grandmother looking on, he visited each piece of play equipment with studied industry, waiting patiently at the foot of the steps to the slide for his turn, reluctant to engage with other children.

Georgie and Cherry would be chatting but also keeping an eye on him. Very frequently he ran back to their laps and stood a while between them, catching strands of their long, winding conversation.

For a good ten years mother and son had something inviolable. They were a very civilised, quiet, empathetic pair, with Georgie getting genuine pleasure from being shown around a Lego castle or wooden garage set. They read together and watched children's TV and all this was possible because Georgie, weighing up her responsibilities and loyalties towards both son and mother, switched to part-time hours when Benjamin was four.

"Usually," said Cherry receiving the news that her daughter would be featuring more in her child's life, "mums work part-time in the first few years and then go back to full-time. Trust you to do things the other way around."

"I'm ready now," said Georgie. "I don't think I could have left before."

She was right. She didn't miss her job half as much as she feared she might and she didn't find childcare a chore. There was a perfection to it all and she savoured it.

Her boy, her beautiful, growing boy. All hers. Sweet, funny, with dark hazel eyes and a wave to his hair. In bed, often before Sam was home from work, he would ask for stories from her youth. She couldn't understand why, having had a perfectly mundane childhood, but after a while she realised it was because she spoke with such a tenderness that it relaxed him and made him trust the idea of distant adulthood, if it was always built on such loving foundations. Her boy, her thoughtful, strong, sure-footed, serious boy.

And then suddenly, he wasn't hers anymore. At fourteen, as his clear skin erupted and hair became lank, as his legs extended into monkey limbs, and his shoulders widened and aligned with his hips to make a preposterous triangle, as his voice struggled to come out over a bed of gravel and his viewing habits became oblique and secret, he detached himself from his mother. He would laugh at her if she couldn't quite express herself, sidle away from her in public, tell her off if he thought she was making a fool of herself. He didn't want to share his inner world with her, let alone with his grandmother, and most of the time wanted to be left alone. Georgie recognised and remembered the struggle, the fear of loving and being loved, the terror of impending responsibility. Sometimes, when no one was looking, he'd give her a rather wooden hug and she felt in that tiny gesture all the agony of growing up and growing away. She wanted to tell him that it wouldn't always be like this, that he was in the clutch of his hormones, but the very mention of hormones would have made him lash out and tell her to leave him alone.

Sam's quiet manliness was what Benjamin needed to get him through. Georgie was relieved that Sam could so effortlessly commune with his teenage son but for a long time she missed him.

"He'll come back," said Cherry. "Everything is as it should be. You and I both know that."

"It was different for us," said Georgie. "Just the two of us. I had nowhere to run and you had no one to hand me over to."

"That's probably why we know each other so well."

"Will I know Benjamin as well?" wondered Georgie aloud.

"That boy is something special," said Cherry. "Full of love and feeling. He's loyal. Lucky girl – or boy – who ends up with him."

"Oh God! I don't want to think about that yet!"

"It's neither here nor there what we think, Georgie girl. These things just happen."

They did, they just happened. Georgie came out of hospital and found a shy young woman in her home wanting to belong to them. Benjamin, 21 years old, seemed to have become the centre of the house, coming and going at all hours, bringing back stories from outside, sure and firm-footed, affectionate with both of his parents but presumably closer now to another person. Yes, he was the loyal type and – unlike in his early youth – brave and confident in the wider world. It was time he went over to his grandmother's house and sorted out this intolerable situation.

As Beatrice lay beside her, the two of them looking at passing clouds through the skylight, both men out, the house utterly silent, Georgie said:

"Do you actually love Benjamin? I mean, are you in love with him?"

The girl said nothing.

"I always wondered how that would feel? To lose your son to another woman. I thought it would be awful. I didn't think I could bear it." She turned her face to Beatrice and grinned. "Turns out I don't mind at all. No big deal."

Beatrice appeared greatly relieved.

"Yes," she said solemnly, "I *am* in love with him. Not quite sure if he's in love with me though."

"Ah."

"So, you probably won't be losing him to me."

Georgie inspected the clear eyes for tears but couldn't find any. There was a strength there. A sign of the extraordinary test of endurance that was having to survive mis-matched love.

"You're a looker-after, aren't you?" said Georgie.

"I suppose I am. It's what makes me happiest, being of help."

"Well," said Georgie, returning to the sky, resting her vision, "there's no way he wouldn't appreciate that. I'll make sure he knows it."

"Please," said Beatrice plaintively, "please, if it's all right, just don't say anything to him about me. It'll only make it worse."

Georgie didn't want to make things worse. She was already sure that she couldn't go a day without this girl. She'd do nothing to send her packing.

*

She called. Sam back at his desk, Benjamin at work on a night shift, Beatrice reading on the bed beside her. She would keep calling until she got an answer. Even if Cherry was going through a blurry patch, having trouble remembering everyone, still there would be moments when Georgie's name would flash up on her phone and she'd make the instant connection with her daughter and answer. Georgie called – she lost count of how many times – and no one answered.

In the early hours, Beatrice gone to bed, the house silent, her phone buzzed.

"Please leave us alone," was the message.

15

It was July, somehow, by the time she emerged into the street.

When she wasn't watching the clouds through the skylight, she was at the bigger window on the other side of the room, with its view of the garden. From here she witnessed the summer swell and erupt, observed the lawn as it yellowed, then browned in the heat. The gardener had come, though very rarely, and Sam only allowed her out on those days when the gardener wasn't there for fear that Georgie would tire herself out trying to give him orders. The first time she sat in the garden was strange. Months had passed, plants had grown, bloomed and shrivelled. She'd missed them. It was criminal to have bypassed such short but gorgeous lives. Once more, it occurred to her that she would like to garden for a living and that she'd like to do it with Cherry. When this was all over, when people could mix again and businesses emerge from their forced inertia, they would grow flowers and sell them. Or something. She'd discuss it with Cherry just as soon as…

"I'm strong enough to go for a walk," she told Sam, who sat opposite her at the garden table, distracted, his phone close to his eyes.

"What?"

"I'm going to go out in the next few days. I'm allowed a walk, aren't I?"

Sam was irritated by a message. "Not alone you're not," he mumbled.

"Of course not. I'll go with..." She surprised herself with her hesitation, feeling she'd said enough. Why did she need his permission anyway?

"Who?" he asked, still absorbed.

"My new friend. Benjamin's girl."

A wavering, it seemed to her, her husband tensing, his attention caught. Something hung in the air, just for that second, something unspoken, and yet it spoke to Georgie.

"I'm not happy with that situation," he said, simply. "We're meant to be in isolation."

Naomi had told her not to care, not to worry. This was all part of the retraining, the stepping aside from petty things. Sam's unhappiness with a situation was not her concern. The house seemed to be running fine without her, in any case. She lived, instead, behind that red door, visited the rooms of her mother's house in her waking and in her sleeping, entering newly vacated spaces, hearing echoes of voices.

"Never mind," she heard herself say. "You're right."

Sam left his phone and his seat and joined her, crouching down in front of her.

"You're looking better, anyway," he said, inspecting her face.

"I feel better."

She did. It only recently occurred to her that she had improved, having woken up for the first time that week without a thought for her breathing or her lungs. There was a new impatience, a raring to go. Her mind was clear and sharp, her movements easier and her mood lifted. Beatrice had got her this far – there was no doubt about it. The young woman had listened and understood, had been infinitely patient with the invalid without pandering to her. Georgie sensed that Beatrice was as keen as she was to get out and re-join the living. The two of them had closely examined the Seasalt website when it became clear that none of Georgie's clothes fitted anymore. They settled on a long, navy blue linen dress which they agreed would be the most practical and would get her through the remainder of the summer. For the rest of the time she wore her pyjamas or a lightweight dressing gown. Even her underwear was too large, her bras laughably hollow and puckered, her pants sagging at the bottom. A Marks & Spencer package had brought her a new set of pants and the kind of relaxed bra tops that she'd always longed to wear but hadn't trusted in the past. A dress and some new underwear, that was all she needed to restore her to the world of the functioning healthy.

Sam was telling her about the lifting of restrictions and how he was expected to go in to work whenever there were press conferences.

"That's not your department though," she said.

"Every department has a stake in this."

She shrugged. "I'll be fine, you know. I'm just going to go as far as Mum's."

"Listen." He was looking at her with some seriousness now. "You might not hear it yourself, but you wheeze a fair bit. I'm worried about your lungs. I can tell that you're shaky. I can see it in you."

What can you possibly hear that I don't, she mused? And she realised that when he talked like this, putting her in her place, she didn't want to confide in him at all. She missed him, missed being able to talk to him. But she wanted to punish him, she didn't know what for. For his paternalistic love? For his love, full stop.

*

"Come on," she said to Beatrice that afternoon. "We're going out."

Beatrice's eyes widened. She sat up on the bed. "Where? Are you sure?"

"The time has come. I want you to meet my mum. I don't need permission from that bastard."

Sam was working in the bedroom office, the door shut. They could hear him having a Zoom meeting. It would last for at least another hour. Georgie knew his meeting schedule well by now, could hear him through the floorboards.

"Oh I don't mean Sam! You needn't look that appalled. Though I don't need his permission either." She was pulling the blue dress over her head, not at all concerned about Beatrice seeing her in her underwear. "I've got some sandals downstairs somewhere." She led the way out of the loft bedroom and, although she'd seemed blasé about Sam, they both still quieted their steps as they passed his room.

The Brake was as exquisite as the first time she had seen it: tranquil and mellow in the full summer glow, sunlight sprinkling through the sycamore leaves. A few neighbours were out, mostly busying themselves with their gardens. Though restrictions had lifted to some extent, people were still reluctant to come too close to each other and The Brake's houses, already so private, felt sacrosanct. That's why she and Sam had fallen in love with the place, because a person could belong and yet not feel obliged to rub shoulders with her neighbours. And it was lovely – loveliness appealing to Sam in particular.

Georgie put her head down and made her way along the street. She felt the tension in her muscles, the rattling of her bones. The way her feet touched down was almost comical, her gait spikey and childlike. Beatrice was keeping behind her as though ready to catch her when she fell. At the end of The Brake, the world arrived. Noisy, busy, ugly. They walked along the carriageway, then crossed it and headed towards the housing estate.

"Are you OK?" Beatrice called.

"Yep." It wasn't quite correct. Her breathing was shallow and her nerves were raw. She felt a little panicked, very exposed. But she kept on and soon she was within minutes of her mother's house. In the sunshine, even the estate had a certain serenity. There was a hush, a baited breath, that she rather treasured and hoped would last. There it was, the little white house, with its neat paintwork and red front door. The tiny strip of front garden was in good order, the pots of white petunias watered and fresh-looking.

"I'll hang back," said Beatrice.

Georgie looked behind her and saw her support retreating but she didn't need her right now. Beatrice was right, she would be a complication. Cherry didn't know her and there was no point in making introductions and confusing her. Georgie arrived at the door and knocked. She stepped back and waited. Somewhere on the estate a car stereo was pounding. It passed and petered out. She knocked again.

"Try again," called Beatrice.

Georgie huffed and tensed. She didn't need to be told.

She knocked harder. Still no response, so she stepped to the side and put her face to the living room window. The room was empty but, looking all the way through it, she could see into the kitchen and through the window at the far end of the kitchen, into the garden. There was her mother, in silhouette. She was sitting in her garden, looking straight ahead of her. Georgie could make out her bobbed hair and the top of her nose.

"Mama," said Georgie under her breath. Then louder: "Mum!" But Cherry didn't turn. She couldn't hear her. Georgie moved back to the door and banged harder. She leant down to the letter box and called her mother. The silence coming from the house was stolid and defiant. It all felt so unwelcoming, so unlike her mother's home. She stepped back and looked up to the front bedroom window. The curtain, it seemed to her, had only a second before shivered back into place.

"Right." Georgie walked back up the path and entered the neighbour's front garden and rang the doorbell. An elderly woman answered.

"Enid!"

"Hello you. How you been, darling? I heard you was ill."

"Much better thank you. You all right?"

Enid hadn't opened the door all the way, clung onto the edge of it as though she might have to shut it very soon.

"I don't like any of this business, do you? You can't put the telly on without all them numbers, people dying and what have you. I don't want to know. Do you?"

Georgie felt the tension ripple in her neck. She and Cherry had always found Enid sweet but tiresome, a lonely widow who feared and distrusted the wider world at the best of times.

"Enid, I'm really sorry to bother you but I wondered if I could just come through into your garden. You see, Mum is at the back and she can't hear me. I just want to have a chat with her."

Enid's expression was scandalised.

"Come through my house?"

"Yes. Please. If that's OK. Maybe she's having a nap and can't hear me."

"You're not allowed, are you? You're not in my bubble."

Oh God, bloody bubbles again.

"I've already had it. You've nothing to worry about."

The scowl on Enid's gaunt face was quite a sight. Georgie wanted to call Beatrice over just to see it.

"You could be contagious all over again."

"I'm not though."

"You could be."

"May I just…"

The door was pushed rapidly forwards, into her face, her progress cut off. Enid's voice could be heard through the reduced gap. "It's not me, love. Nothing personal. It's the rules."

"Then could you please just call over your fence and tell my mum that I'm here and to open the door for me."

The door closed. Georgie waited. After a while she returned to her mother's living room window and looked through it. Cherry was no longer in the garden. There was no sign of anyone anywhere. Georgie sat down on the doorstep. She could just about make out Beatrice hovering on the other side of the small square, between a bush and a bin. The girl made a gesture to ask what was up. Georgie shrugged and shook her head. More minutes passed. Georgie's mouth felt very dry. Why hadn't she brought some water with her? She got up and banged on the door.

"Mum! For God's sake."

There was a solid mass of anger building, though she wasn't at all sure who she was furious at. Someone. The someone who hid behind curtains, the someone who kept her locked out. The keys! She had a set of keys for the house. Why didn't she think to bring them? But she was too tired to go and come back again.

She beat her fists on the door. She knew he was there. He was stopping her mother coming out to see her. She saw in her mind her mother's profile again, the sense of vacantness. Was she happy? The tears were threatening. Where was Cherry? Could she hear her daughter?

"Mum! Please."

She didn't even know his name. Who the hell was he? What right did he have?

"I'm going to call the police," she called out to him.

Enid's door was open, her sparrow face in the crack. "Best you go home, love. Come back tomorrow."

Still Georgie knocked, ignoring the neighbour. She knocked and she coughed at the same rate and suddenly her legs weakened and she leant against the door, panting. Beatrice was beside her, her soft, calm voice in Georgie's ear. "That lady's right. Maybe go home. We'll come back with the keys. We should have thought of the keys."

"Why didn't I think of the keys? I was an idiot."

"You're looking shaky."

"She's in there. I'm so close. Why can't I just see her?"

Enid was still talking from behind her door.

"She's very well looked after. Don't you worry. A load off your mind."

Georgie glanced up to find the source of the words.

"Enid, who is he? Who *is* he?"

The old lady pulled a face.

"Oh I don't know his name, my love. You look all tired out. Go home. Best thing."

"She's right," said Beatrice. "Come on. We'll come back."

"I'm going to tell the police. This isn't right."

"Home."

They stumbled back across the square and just as she reached the other end, Georgie looked back and was convinced once again that the curtains were being replaced, that a hand was just disappearing.

This was hate. This was the blunt, shapeless enmity that was – remarkably – still growing. She was angry with him, and she was furious with her mother who insisted on picking up waifs and strays and getting herself embroiled in other people's pathetic lives. A loser. A hanger-on. The kind of parasite that finds himself a host and convinces himself that he is finally of value to the world. He wasn't. He was worthless and she would come straight back and turf him out. All she had to do was find the keys.

*

Going up the stairs to the loft finished her off. She lay on the bed and felt the tremble in her core, which fanned out into a consistent shaking of the limbs and finally a convulsion. She was having a panic attack. She knew it. She could be logical even in her panic. Great waves of shaking ran through her and she waited, wide-eyed, sweating, for the tremors to die back. Beatrice must have told Sam because he was leaning over her, his forehead deeply furrowed, his teeth locked together, liked he was witnessing a fight, unable to step in and quell it.

When it was over, he put on the TV and they sat together in silence, his arm around her, her head on his shoulder.

She went to sleep early, afraid that the breathlessness would come back, that the rusty chain would return in her dreams, and all the visions of a clouded, sick mind that she didn't want to see again. Afraid that she would have to go back to hospital if she didn't learn how to reduce all her mental and physical outgoings to the slightest and most essential. Afraid that she was losing control all over again.

*

Late at night, she awoke to find Beatrice sitting beside her.

"You're awake?"

"What do you want, Beatrice?" she asked.

The girl knelt down and, with their noses virtually touching, she spoke is a low, gentle murmur.

"I have to go home. I can't stay any longer."

Georgie felt pained. She remembered Sam in the garden, the colour rising to his cheeks.

"Is it my fault? Did they tell you off?"

"No, they didn't say anything. But my family needs me. I can't stay away for ever."

"Will you come back?"

"Yes, yes of course. They seem to think there'll be another lockdown and then, well, I hope Benjamin will want me with him again. He is so loving, you know, so keen to do the right thing by everyone, but he's still very young in a way, a bit selfish, but that's all right, that's fine. I know how people work."

Georgie closed her mouth in an effort to control her breaths. The moon was bright and the room was tinged with silver. The girl's almond cream skin was luminous.

"So, you'll come back?"

"Definitely."

Georgie felt her body loosen and her eyelids lower. She was content.

"You'll be fine. I know it. You had a bit of a set-back but you're getting stronger and stronger. You're heading the right way. Get lots of fresh air and build yourself up. When I come back we can choose some more clothes for you. You can't wear the same blue dress forever, you know."

That was rich – Georgie smiled to herself – for a young woman who had lived in the same outfit for as long as Georgie had known her. In the moonlight, the sparse, purpled clouds strolling across the skylight, the room was their perfect world, her anchorage. She opened her eyes a little later and Beatrice was already gone.

16

The police officer had a woman's name but a man's voice. It baffled Georgie and for the first minute of the call she found herself struggling to make herself clear. Or that's how it felt, the policewoman coming across as politely sceptical but perhaps actually non-plussed. It was having to talk formally to someone again that led to this blurring. Georgie's thoughts, as ever, turned inside, and found gaps and spaces, the barely audible and the unreachable. By the time she returned, a question had been asked and PC Leah Hitchin was waiting for a response.

"Are you able to answer, Mrs Greenfield? Do you have reason to believe that your mother may be at risk of harm?"

Was Cherry in danger? The rationalist in Georgie wanted to bat the suggestion away. Of course not. She saw her mother in the boutique, dealing with difficult customers, brushing off rudeness, unperturbed by them. Georgie – easily offended and rattled by bad behaviour – had always marvelled at how easily her mother righted herself after any confrontation. But then, the old Cherry, the real one, was slowly disappearing before her daughter's eyes.

"My mother had mild dementia which suddenly speeded up. They said it might be a tumour and were going to do tests but then all this happened and I had to go to hospital and I've no idea if she's had any appointments. The prognosis was not fantastic. She needs me with her to help her grasp even the most ordinary things. Don't get me wrong, sometimes she's perfectly normal but at other times she just doesn't understand what's going on."

"And she's not able to stay with you?"

"Like I said, I've been ill. I didn't know if I was coming or going."

"I'm sorry to hear that, Mrs Greenfield."

"I can barely look after myself at the moment."

The scene at Cherry's front door yesterday had unquestionably set her back. She didn't want Sam to know what had taken place and had sworn Beatrice to secrecy. But she felt adrift and anaemic. Enfeebled again, she feared illness with a new and surprising terror. She had lost all trust in her body.

"But there's someone with her?"

"Yes, that's the point. I don't know who he is. He's much younger than her. He won't let me talk to her on the phone and he won't let me into her house."

"She owns the property?"

"Yes."

Where was Beatrice? She needed a witness to everything. That was the legal basis. Corroboration.

The officer seemed to be humming to herself, in a gravelly baritone, was making notes presumably. Georgie couldn't bear to hear it.

"I'll go back today. Try and get his name. Is that what you need? Then you can look him up."

The distant grating hum continued. Georgie waited.

"What? No, don't do that," said the officer suddenly, waking up. "Let me go and assess things. I'll let you know. When did you last see your mother?"

"Yesterday. I could see her through the window. She didn't hear me."

"And she appeared normal to you?"

Georgie was seeing Cherry again, a familiar profile, a face turned away from her, looking into the distance. Perhaps not looking at all. Seeming insentient.

"No. I mean, yes, in a way. But no, not right. She would have answered the door if she was right."

"And this man was there with her?"

"He was hiding upstairs."

The pause, the hum, the delay of information-capture. Georgie tipped back her head and concentrated on her breathing. The eventual re-joining: "You'll appreciate we're even busier than normal at the moment."

"I thought," said Georgie, trying to be sensitive, fouling it up as ever, "that you'd be *less* busy. Everyone at home, including the criminals."

"People either don't want to be at home or don't get the rules." The police officer's involuntary little sigh humanised her and brought a woman at last to Georgie's mind. Was it too late to appeal to her as a daughter? Should one appeal to officers in any case?

"So please be patient," continued PC Hitchin. "If I can't get back to you later today then it'll be tomorrow. But I'll definitely look into it. Let's not worry until we know what's what."

Georgie let the phone drop onto the duvet and instantly picked up the TV remote. If there were hours that needed filling then, perhaps Sam was right, the television could do it.

*

The call came the following morning at just after eight. Georgie had messaged Sam to ask if she could have her breakfast in bed, that she felt a little drained. He had only just laid the tray on her lap when her phone rang. Sam hovered by the door while she took the call. It irritated her to be listened to as she tried to speak coherently.

"There was no one there," said PC Hitchin.

"Sorry?"

"I went at five thirty in the evening and knocked on the door and no one answered."

"That's what I said! He won't open the door to me."

"It seemed that the property was empty."

"The property is *not* empty."

"It seemed that way to me."

Sam, watching Georgie intently from the doorway, appeared uptight. She shook her head, wanted him to leave her alone.

"Would you like me to try again?" asked the officer.

Georgie's energy was dwindling already, so early in the day.

"Yes, yes, I would. But I bet you won't."

"I'd like to resolve this."

"So would I!"

Sam was moving forward, his expression full of questions. Georgie waved him away.

"We've logged the call. I'm going off duty but I'll make sure an officer sees these notes and calls you back."

"Calls me back why, exactly?"

The phone was being taken from her hands and Sam was retreating with it onto the landing. Her nerves were screaming. When he came back, she was watching the television resolutely and didn't wish to talk to him. He placed the phone on the duvet and left the room.

*

Darkness. Another day gone. It made her depressed to think of all the time that was disappearing behind her. She had spent the entire day in front of a burbling screen, her meals brought to her, husband and son coming in occasionally to check her over, plant a kiss and retreat. They were beyond solicitous, their saddened eyes turned towards her like they were meandering cattle passing through. She was growing tired of their tenderness, increasingly embarrassed about her dependency on them. Only Beatrice knew how to make her feel normal. Sam and Benjamin seemed so scared of her at times, like the worst was not behind but ahead of them.

And then, of course, it always changed and she needed them at night, when she woke and knew they were unreachable. That was the loneliest time for her.

Georgie slept with the keys to her mother's house under her pillow. Just as soon as she could – when that feeling of exhaustion dissipated, when her calm returned – she would be fitting them in the lock and opening the red door. Cherry would be there, welcoming her in. He, the Youngster, would have gone by then. Maybe he already wasn't there. Cherry would have booted him out, the irritating, self-righteous sponger. And then what? A walk to the park? Maybe. But maybe just a moment to look at each other and assess what had happened to them in the long blank of their recent separation. They could tell each other everything, the very smallest things even, pick up on the subtle gradations of ageing, showing in their faces, seeping through their conversation. "I'm sorry," Georgie would say, "I'm sorry about my brattish behaviour as a child. I didn't mean to hurt you." She would wait to hear the instant, warm dismissal. "You were not a brat, Georgie girl. We had the best of lives."

Of all memories, Georgie couldn't dispel one from her earliest days in secondary school when she would go to the boutique after school to sit in the storeroom at the back and wait for her mother to close up. She was thirteen years old and easily embarrassed and uncomfortable among adults. Nestled under a rail of dresses and jackets, only her legs visible under all the fabric, she listened to the ebbing and flowing talk of the customers and her mother. Cherry was adept at using conversation to hold on to the shop's visitors, keep them from turning around and leaving, was unabashed about discussing what seemed to her daughter to be the most private of details. Even as Cherry listened, she contributed. There was a skill to it, a beautiful mystery. And, just as Georgie resented all adult skills that she didn't understand, she was scornful of this one.

"Why are you giving them advice?" she asked her mother once as they walked home.

"It's not advice. It's fellow feeling."

"But you don't have a husband so what do *you* know?"

Cherry paused only the briefest moment, as she often did to recover. "People like to know that you're interested in their lives. And I am. I'm very interested."

"But you don't go all silly about men like they do. You don't need a husband. You don't want all that, all the stuff that they complain about."

"I don't know what I need, Georgie."

"You need me."

Georgie had been flustered, then sullen. There was nothing more to be said.

"Yes," said her mother. "You're right. I need you."

Cherry Weston, striking, poised, exceptional Cherry Weston. Full of energy, often mischievous, wanting to live, live, live. Men were extraneous. They could never be good enough for her. And now her daughter lay with her mother's door keys under her pillow, waiting for the coast to clear so that she could open the red front door and come to a stop at last, resting in her mother's presence, re-joined and where she should be.

*

The earliest birds. A neighbour's car door slamming.

Feet on the stairs, doors opening and closing. Voices.

We can't tell her. Not yet.

When?

When she's stronger.

The bin lorry roars up the road and the voices are eaten up and lost. Silence after.

17

She knocked on the door a couple of times as a formality and then put the tip of the key in place. It was an overcast day, the clouds very low, the air heavy and hot. She couldn't quite get the key to go all the way into the Yale lock. She pulled it out and stared at it. Had she brought the wrong key? The idiot. No, no it had to be the right one. It was the same key chain. It was right, definitely right. Once again, she tried to push it all the way into the slot but it wouldn't go. She jammed it, cursed it, wriggled it. Then she stepped back and examined the lock. Around its edge was a newly applied patch of red paint. And the lock itself was pristine, entirely new.

With the heel of her hands, she jabbed at the door, setting it shivering on its hinges. Something was rising in her, coming up through her chest, pushing out of her, something that threatened to overwhelm her. It was like she might fire out a cannonball at any minute, the pressure building, the explosion imminent.

Under her breath, she was reciting: "Fucking open the door. Open it. Open it now."

Rising, rising. Some kind of malevolent strength was coming. As though silence were for the weakest, those unable to help themselves. Coming up and out of her, the explosion.

"Open it now!"

She stepped back, her chest heaving. Was he there? Was he watching from behind the curtain and smiling?

"Let her out!" she cried. "Give her back. Give her back to me."

She was conscious of coughing. Maybe she'd been hacking like this all along, but it was only now that it was obstructing her voice that she noticed it. But she would scream around the coughs.

"Give her back. Give her back right now." She flew at the door, barged it, was crying openly. "Mama, come out. Let her out, you bastard."

Just as she raised her right arm to smash it against the door once more, she felt it being grasped and pulled down to her side.

"Mum, Mum. Sh. Stop it. Come on. Come home."

She turned her head and, confused, saw Benjamin, his expression wide-eyed and aghast.

"I'm not leaving," she told her son. "This has gone on long enough. He's changed the bloody lock. Can you believe that?"

Benjamin was putting his arm around her and trying to guide her away from Cherry's house. Georgie saw Sam arriving.

"I told you," Benjamin said bitterly to his father. "We should have told her straight away, as soon as we knew."

"Come home, Geeny," said Sam. "Please. Your mum's not here."

"She is!" insisted Georgie. "He's stopping me from seeing her. I don't know why. But I won't leave."

"Please...please." Sam was now at her other side and, between husband and son, she was being manoeuvred back in the direction of The Brake. As they walked, Georgie's breaths came sharply out of her, and at speed. Sam was shaking his head. Benjamin was containing himself.

She cried as she spoke to them.

"I just want to know she's all right. I want to see her." It appeared to be the most pitiful comment ever made because even her husband, staid, steady, unflappable Sam, looked like he was damming up an inevitable flood of emotion.

*

She sat between them on the bench at the back of the garden. Each man had claimed one of her hands. It was late afternoon and the weather was threatening to break, the clouds inky and morose. On the brief walk home, Georgie, cowed, had said nothing. Sam and Benjamin were speechless, too. Each time she stopped to catch her breath they would wait and look on.

They led her directly to the garden, Benjamin running to get the cushions from the shed, Sam depositing her, then fetching more lemon barley water from the house. They watched her drink it. She felt over-burdened by their attention but unable to ask them to leave her alone. She didn't want this degree of care and concern. It unnerved her.

"I'm fine now," she said after a while. "I'm going to bed."

"Gina," said Sam.

She turned to him, suspicious of his tone. It was compassionate but nervous. His expression was pained. She looked next at her son. He, too, was agitated. Benjamin flexed his lips, hesitated, mumbled "Mum".

"What is it?" she asked them.

Sam spoke, his words dropping unevenly from him.

"Your mother's partner came over late last night. Alan. He

wanted us to know that your mother was ill. Suddenly ill. Anyway…"

"What? Ill with what?"

"Geeny…" She felt the grip tighten on both hands at the same time.

"What?"

"I rang the hospital this morning and I'm desperately, desperately sorry to say that she was…or she just had…passed away. I'm…"

"No," said Georgie, smartly, sure of herself. "It's a lie. That man's lying."

She looked to her son for support.

"Mum. It's true. They said it was a stroke. I'm sorry. We wanted to tell you this morning but you were asleep and we didn't know how strong you were and…"

A stroke. Cherry Weston had died of a stroke. No. No, it wasn't true. It wasn't the way. This was not a fitting end. She hadn't ended. Not this way. Not being told on a garden bench with the full awkwardness of your husband and son, but sitting beside her, holding her hand, laughing gently at stories from their shared past. That was the plan. Anyway, Georgie had seen her through the window in the garden only a few days before. She wasn't gone. This was a mistake. She looked from husband to son, son to husband, the exact same sorrowful emptiness, nothing more to say, bracing themselves.

There was simply no way that it could be true. The idea was failing to penetrate. What did they want her to say? She wasn't having it and, besides, they were out of their minds believing anything that awful man said.

"He's not my mother's partner," she told them categorically. "And he's changed the locks."

18

For days she wouldn't talk to them. She wanted them to know that she blamed them entirely for what had happened. Her anger rose when one of them entered the loft bedroom and he would hover for a moment and retreat. She ate alone, her food in her lap, usually sitting at the back of the garden, on the very bench where they'd imparted the news of Cherry's death. On one occasion Sam dared to suggest that she might want to sit somewhere else, that there would be too many bad associations for her with that bench. They would get rid of it.

"No, you won't," she snapped back. "How can you not understand?"

She wanted those bad associations. She wanted to relive the shock of the news of Cherry's death every time she sat on it. None of it was to slip away, not a single second of that hideous revelation. It was incised into the wood. She would sit on that moment every day, remember every word uttered by her and her husband and son. Recall their stupefied expressions.

"You need time to mourn, Mum," Benjamin had said, his arm around her shoulder.

What did this child know about mourning? Was he seriously suggesting that she should start the whole process of letting go? She was nowhere near grieving yet.

"I've been thinking, Geeny." It was Sam's turn to be solicitous. "When you're strong enough – maybe at some point tomorrow or the day after – we'll call on this Alan chap and ask him about the funeral. Sorry to bring that up so early. And see what we can do to help."

It was like freezing. Suddenly stopping. Or maybe more like electrocution. Every nerve died at that moment. And then she had to restart herself all over again.

"See what we can do to help?" she asked, her voice reduced to a gritty whisper. "To *help*?"

Sam was struggling.

"I just felt that seeing as he'd looked after her for so long now and that you're still not fully recovered, we could work together on this. He certainly intimated that he had everything in hand."

"Dad, no." Benjamin had understood the situation better than his father.

"Sorry."

That's why she wouldn't talk to them, couldn't even bring herself to ask them for Beatrice's number. She would give them nothing of herself.

Georgie rang the hospital that night but couldn't get anything sensible from anyone. No one seemed to know what she was talking about and she was even rebuked at one point by a ward nurse who told her there "happens to be a pandemic on".

In the morning, she called Cherry's GP and waited on the line for nearly half an hour, the receptionist cutting through every few minutes to say that Dr Croft was very busy due to the situation.

"I'm happy to come and see her face-to-face," said Georgie.

The receptionist was scandalised at the very thought.

Eventually Dr Croft answered and before Georgie could say anything she offered her condolences, explaining that the hospital had emailed the details to the patient's surgery.

"I don't know anything about it," said Georgie. "Literally nothing."

Georgie could picture her mother's doctor, her short dark curls, perennial uniform of black lace blouse and pearls, her swollen-looking fingers ending in sharp red nails. Cherry had always referred to her as Dr Frank-N-Furter.

Dr Croft was talking about having to fill in the death certificate and getting it to the registrar as soon as possible. It was a rehearsed speech. Georgie couldn't stomach it.

"Had she been to see you? Was she with *him*?"

"There's only so much I can tell you, patient confidentiality..."

"My mother has died. There's no confidentiality."

"There *is* confidentiality but as it happens there's nothing I think she'd wish to keep from you. But you must understand, Mrs Greenfield, that she was slipping away very fast, or her mind was. It was very distressing for her. Vascular dementia and strokes go hand-in-hand."

"Why wasn't I told?"

"Her partner knew. I assumed it was all getting back to you."

"It wasn't. I didn't know anything. I don't know why everyone is calling him her partner, for that matter."

The doctor was evidently uncomfortable. Georgie could hear the red nails tapping on a keyboard.

"So…looking at my notes, I see that she came here with her… with *him* on April the fourteenth this year following scans at the hospital. She was lucky to get an appointment, given the way things were going then. We discussed the results of the scan which were…"

"What?"

"That the rapid onset dementia could have been caused by a subdural haematoma. A blood clot in the brain. It can lead to an atrophy."

Georgie repeated the words silently several times.

"I didn't know. Nobody told me."

"Well, that's…that's tragic. I'm sorry."

Georgie's voice was catching now, the blockage in her throat expanding.

"How was she? How did she seem to you?"

"I remember," said Dr Croft, her voice vague with revisiting the moment. "We said we couldn't see patients face-to-face because of the virus. But we made exceptions. She was one of them. She was quiet. He did all the talking."

"What? What was he saying?"

"I'm afraid I can't recall. He wanted to know what he could do, I think. What she should take. He came across as very concerned, I remember that. Almost tearful. I don't really feel comfortable telling you those details."

Comfortable? Georgie examined the word and discarded it. Why was the doctor's comfort any concern of hers?

"Did you know that she was going to die?"

Dr Croft said nothing. There was no tapping of the keyboard, just empty air.

"Please, that's all I'm asking. Did you know that she was going to die?"

"No one knows that kind of thing for sure. It's not like she had cancer or a weak heart. These things are often operable. But..." The doctor paused, was struggling. "We did discuss end-of-life, yes."

"Did she understand?"

"How can I answer that?"

"Did she understand?"

"No. I don't think she did."

"I haven't finished with this," said Georgie and put the phone down.

*

Georgie went to Sam's room and told him she was fine and that he should go to work and help with the press conference.

He got up from his desk and came over and put his arms around her.

"I am so sorry that you're going through this. And now, at such a difficult time. I know you're suffering enormously."

Georgie looked beyond his shoulder at the desk, at his abeyant phone and tablet, his laptop open on a half-written email, and she wondered if Beatrice had ever come in to talk to him. Asked if he wanted a cup of tea perhaps. Offered to do some chore or other. Had that gentle calming presence ever stood in his doorway and listened to his work woes?

"I wish she was here," she said.

"I know, I know."

He pulled back to inspect her face, kissed her. "We can still give her a good send-off. Even if the numbers are restricted. Thirty of her friends and family. We can do that. Maybe you should go and make your peace with her bloke. He'll want to be involved, I'm sure."

She freed herself from him. This is what came of opening up even slightly to Sam.

"I was talking about Beatrice," she said and left the room.

*

In the dark, alone, at night, she cried. She saw Cherry chatting with customers at the boutique, dropping her head back and laughing heartily. She saw her as she would have seen her once long ago, looking up at her as they sat beside each other in the bus heading into the West End for a treat: the department stores and a restaurant in Soho. Always side-by-side – walking home from Annika's or taking the bus – glued together.

Her face hot, the tears even hotter, Georgie remembered walking with Cherry in the park, stopping to enjoy the moorhens on the pond, the conversation softly nudging towards Cherry's memory problems, discussing the upcoming hospital scan, being rather innocent and philosophical about the whole thing. Whatever happened, they said, they would be together. But now there was a mist of sleep and sorrow that veiled her mother's face and Georgie called to Cherry, begged her to come back.

Mama. Please...I want to see you again.

The face in the mist was neither young nor old, was the essence of her mother, the momentary bright stamp of a rapidly receding life.

*

When she awoke, she saw a figure in the doorway.

Georgie's eyes were sore and her vision patchy in the morning half-light.

"They asked if I'd come back and look after you for a while," said Beatrice.

"I can't bear the thought that she might have suffered or was scared or…or was asking for me and didn't understand why I wasn't there."

The girl stepped forward and her smile seemed to soften the air around her.

"We'll get through this. I promise."

19

There were some fractious years of employment – as there are for anyone – and Georgie and her colleagues once found themselves taking part in a team-building weekend at a conference centre outside Colchester. Georgie had sat quietly at the back during workshops, contributing little though pondering much. Kyle was the name of the earnest young man who ran the sessions. If anything brought that team of government lawyers together on that dire weekend it was their collective distaste for the way Kyle wore his lime green shirt open one button too low, with surprisingly many sandy hairs protruding in a way that suggested that he'd hidden a Yorkshire terrier down his front.

"What's your proudest moment?" he asked them the last time they were together. "Don't give it too much thought. I don't want a clever answer, just an honest one. A moment of great pride. Georgina – we haven't heard from you yet."

She did as she was told, let herself be spontaneous. It was the day she and her mother had finished transforming the small space at the back of Cherry's house, she informed them. The last of the rubble had gone and Cherry had laid a very small courtyard of flagstones surrounded by narrow beds, with Georgie mixing the cement. As it set, they went to the garden centre and chose pots and plants and came home to devise the planting scheme. Cherry had stood back and admired a layout suggested by her daughter and been genuinely pleased and surprised by Georgie's thinking. That, she told her colleagues, was when she suddenly realised what it was to be proud, to have elicited such a response from someone who had much better taste in garden design. She remembered the feeling: her chest stretching out, her shoulders stiffening.

Georgie's colleagues had listened politely then gone on to give their own accounts, nearly every single one of them citing their roles in drafting the Human Rights Act of 1998. They must have thought she felt foolish, had mis-read what was required of her. But it didn't matter, because she didn't care what they thought. She was lost in consternation because until that moment she hadn't realised quite how deeply such moments as the one with Cherry had meant to her. Why hadn't she acknowledged them at the time? One day, she reasoned, sitting there in the conference centre, she would be looking back on them and taking all her sustenance from them. Was it possible, she wondered, to appreciate all those tiny, perfect domestic moments at the very time they were happening, or did they only exist as memories, straining at her heart, creating a sense of longing? Could all filial love only be recognised in hindsight?

*

When they sat together in the park, they laughed – invariably – about something wicked to do with someone they knew. Their humour came from all the excessive characters they had come across singly or together. Not that wicked, come to think of it.

Entertaining. Cherry's neighbour, Enid, when she looked through everyone's bins, "just in case, my darling". Or the most stuck-up of Georgie's colleagues, complaining that she hadn't been shown due deference by support staff.

Clownish people passed before their eyes, reduced to a line of gossip or a strange mannerism. Old men shuffling with studied concentration, stopping to throw a wave to Cherry. Families in their ragged excess, all familiar with this elegant older lady, acknowledging her with a quick smile. Her "boyfriends", giving her a wink and a knowing nudge.

All our lives lead up to now.

The ultimate now, that's what she'd talked about the last time they had been together. Georgie tried to picture her mother in all her simple loveliness, acknowledging other people's greetings with grace and generosity. But, lying in bed, enveloped in darkness, she couldn't help but grasp the now, the end. She saw Cherry as one of those stone effigies, the wife of a knight, recumbent in an old church, her hands folded elegantly on her chest, her eyes trained up to the ceiling. All the softness gone but the beauty captured for ever.

*

"We'll wait for him," said Georgie. "He's got to leave the house at some point and then we'll just catch up with him and confront him that way."

They were on the bench at the back of the garden. The day was warm but had started damply and would end that way. The summer was winding up.

"Might he be aggressive, do you think?" asked Beatrice.

"Aggressive? I don't think so. Oh because he's lost his meal ticket and his free accommodation? I dare say he'll want to suck up to me. Before this I wanted to know who he was, his name, age, all those details. Now I just want him to understand that he's got to get lost and leave us alone. I'd rather not talk to him but if it comes to legal involvement down the line then at least I can say I've been straight with him. I wonder if we should be recording any conversations with him. What do you think?"

Beatrice peered out at Georgie from under a thick flap of hair that had fallen across her left eye.

"He's like a tramp, isn't he? Do you think he's a drug addict?"

"No, I think he's a loser. I think he's one of those people who can't look after himself and so he's attached himself to someone who..."

"Oh Georgie. Don't. Don't go there."

Georgie turned to Beatrice, her features struggling under constraint. "Don't think about her last moments?" she asked. "Don't speculate on what it was like?" The tears wouldn't be held back. "I wasn't with her, Bea. I wasn't there. And I loved her so much."

"I know."

"But even *I* didn't know how much, so how can you? You can't understand it. Not you, nor Sam, nor Benjamin. It's something that grew up from our past. From the start it was just me and her. I knew it would end – of course it would end – but it would end the way it started. With us. No one else."

Beatrice was evidently pained. She was looking straight ahead of her now, seeing something distasteful. "That bastard," she said and it was so brutal, the way it came out, that Georgie felt a dismal smile form on her lips. It was just one more thing to be angry about – the darkening of such a sweet soul.

"But he'll see us, won't he? Standing outside the house. He won't come out."

"I've thought about that," said Georgie. "We'll drive and then just sit in the car and wait."

"Are you allowed to drive? I'm not sure Sam would be happy…"

"It's a two-minute journey. It'll be fine. It's just somewhere to hide out, as it were."

"A stake-out kind of thing?"

If that's what it takes, thought Georgie. *If that's the way I have to behave, then so be it.*

*

It felt good to be driving again. "Now I know why so many women love the freedom of car ownership," said Georgie and she took them on a little detour of twenty minutes, up into Orpington and then back through the north end of the estate via Broom Hill. They parked in a street that ran round the corner from Cherry's house. From there they could just see if the front door was opened and if someone emerged.

Georgie spoke very little as they sat in the car, let her mind be washed over with Beatrice's babble. It felt almost like the chatter was coming from her own mind, it was so pervasive. She couldn't even catch on to what any of it was about, thought she heard references to her family and to hospitals and the strain on the health service. Finally, Beatrice managed to get Georgie's attention.

"I think maybe Benjamin is destined for a better person than me."

"What on earth do you mean?" Georgie sat up in the driving seat and glared at her companion. "What's wrong with you? You're not getting all humble again, are you? Benjamin's bloody lucky to have you."

Beatrice was unmoved. "It's all right. I'm not feeling sorry for myself. I'm being realistic. I'm not a dynamic kind of person."

"So?"

"So, he's going to do well in the world. He'd be bored with me. Really, don't think I'm complaining. I'm happy to be with him now."

"Why would he be with you if he didn't like you?"

Not for the first time, Beatrice came across as the more mature of the two of them, certainly the more thoughtful.

"Because I'll do. No, no, don't shake your head. You know it's true. You must have thought it. I'm physically reassuring for him. Someone to hold at night. Someone who will listen and say all the right things. Agree with him, tell him he's right. I'm a stage in his life. But that's useful, you know. That gives me purpose. I'll go when the time's right and leave him free. That's what he needs, freedom. To grow, to become someone."

Georgie wanted to contradict the girl but found she couldn't. There had always seemed something slightly preposterous about this pairing and she'd assumed it was sexually convenient. But that wouldn't have been enough for her son. He needed someone combative, stimulating.

"He's like me," said Georgie quietly.

"I think he is."

"So certain about the world. So sure of himself. But with something missing. Not a little thing but a great big demanding thing. I know what he wants…he wants to be left alone and yet he can't bear to be alone."

Beatrice's smile was meant to bolster but seemed so pitying.

"It's not a bad thing, you know, to be the dominant half of the relationship. It's like you're sheltering someone under your wing. You'll do the fighting for them. And in return…"

"And in return, you make us human."

The sun was at its highest and the car was heating up rapidly. Georgie had been looking out of the side window at the red door of her mother's house. Cherry had been the abiding, humanising presence in her life. Everyone knew their place and fell into their roles...but what if one of those players was taken away? Removed before she'd had time to impart the secrets of self-reliance. There had been years – not many but some – where they had been apart from each other and, although both had flourished in their careers, neither had felt complete. It was a curse as well as a blessing to have grown up so loved and cared-for by a parent. Georgie had always feared for her own child when the time came for him or her to leave. It had seemed kinder to set up the parameters first, to ration the love.

"There's still time," said Beatrice tenderly.

"Time for what?" Georgie's voice came out cracked and weak.

"To share the burden with Benjamin. To help him and let him help you."

Georgie closed her eyes and drifted, her mind swimming with images almost as bizarre as the ones she had seen at her most ill and when unconscious. Her feet slipping beneath her, a hand failing to reach her. People floating past. It was a fantastic sight, her waking dreamworld. Was she still unwell? Was she ever well?

She opened her eyes and watched as the front door of her mother's house opened and a pale, thin man emerged, glanced up at the sky and then set off in the direction of the park.

20

"Excuse me!"

The Youngster stopped and waited. He didn't turn around.

They had been walking directly behind him all the way to the edge of the park, letting him cross the main road first, dodging the traffic to cross immediately after him. When he got to the park gates he wrong-footed them, turned towards the high street. If they didn't stop him then he'd be unstoppable, lost to shops and pedestrians.

Georgie trotted to catch up with him and manoeuvred around him, faced him.

The Youngster was not so young after all, maybe in his late forties, maybe a little younger. It was hard to tell. He was dressed in thick grey jeans with creases down the fronts, a blue checked shirt and white trainers. He wore aviator glasses and his hair was longish, greyish and dirtyish. A dome of a belly protruded over his belt. His hands were restless and fluttered around his waist, looking for a perch.

"And you are?"

His voice was as thin as his mouth. She felt sick at the sight of him.

"You know who I am."

"I'm afraid I don't."

Georgie checked behind her and saw that Beatrice was, as always, retreating. Did she do it out of delicacy or fear? Maybe she was embarrassed, expected fireworks.

Georgie was feeling perfectly resolute and needed no one.

"I'm Cherry Weston's daughter. You've been a guest of my mother for a while."

"Oh," he said. "Of course. I thought I recognised your voice."

"I'm pretty certain you've seen me from the top window of my mother's house. But never mind. I need to discuss a few things with you before you leave. Unless you've already moved out, of course."

"Moved out?" His lips were forming something like a quizzical smile. He tapped the side of his face with a finger. She found him repellent.

"Look, I don't want to be unfriendly, but you haven't exactly been easy to contact. I had no idea that she was so unwell, so fragile." Georgie turned her face away from him so that he wouldn't see her distress. She scanned the distant high street as she talked. "My mother and I were very close. It would have upset her not to have me near her. Why did you change the locks?"

"Are you going to be shouty and aggressive again?" he asked.

She turned her gaze back on him.

"I beg your pardon?"

It felt like he was moving away.

"I wanted to protect her," he said.

"Protect her from *me*?"

He was definitely moving away. Small steps, as though he was afraid of her. But he wasn't afraid, couldn't have been. He was playing the part of a victim.

"That's all I wanted to do, keep her safe. No disturbances. It wasn't good for her."

Georgie was laughing, small puffs that juddered out of her.

"Are you seriously saying that you locked me out of my mother's house for her good? I'm going to report this, you know. I want you out of there."

The Youngster said nothing, continued the tiny steps away from her.

"I don't even know your name."

"I've never kept it from you," he said. "I've done nothing to you. Nothing. Why are you so hysterical?"

She stopped, thought about it. She wasn't being hysterical. Not in the slightest. And yet everything seemed to be turning in the wrong direction. Was he right? Was she coming across as unstable? Was she the aggressor after all? Where was Beatrice to hear all this nonsense? To record it. Slowly, with restraint, she told him what she wanted from him.

"I am going to organise my mother's funeral and you are of course welcome but then I would like you to give me the keys to the house and then to leave. Do you have somewhere else to go? If I can be of any help in that regard, then of course I will."

The Youngster shook his head.

"I don't think so," he said and turned his back on her.

She watched him for a stunned moment and then took off after him.

"Excuse me. I haven't finished. Where are you going?"

He was hurrying, looking over his shoulder.

"Leave me alone, please," he said through tight lips.

"Stop!"

Should she run after him?

Beatrice was suddenly there.

"What's going on?"

"He's acting like I'm harassing him."

"I don't like the look of him."

"He's revolting."

They watched the Youngster as he jogged towards the high street, his arms flat against his thighs, his head snapping left and right, as though he thought he might be pounced upon.

"Let him go," said Beatrice. "I think he wants a scene. He's provoking you."

Georgie watched the curious sight of the retreating Youngster, a flimsy pastiche of male humanity, running like someone who was completely new to it.

"There's absolutely no way that my mother would have anything to do with that creep. I'm getting him out of that house before the week is out. I mean it."

*

In the afternoon, they talked about the Youngster, his appearance, his manner. They discussed how it would be best to extricate him, how they could block him from the funeral. Georgie was sitting on her bed with Beatrice beside her and they were searching for legal advice on her laptop.

"Funny isn't it, you being a lawyer and yet needing to look up legal things."

"I'm as clueless as you on this. It's like asking a heart surgeon to do an ear canal operation."

Downstairs the door slammed. Benjamin was back from work. He was doing day shifts and coming home at three. Beatrice sat up and listened.

"I'd better go," she said.

Georgie wondered if Beatrice felt she had to be there to greet her boyfriend as soon as he came home. Or maybe she was being discreet. Benjamin usually came straight upstairs to check on his mother and perhaps Beatrice felt uncomfortable hanging around. The girl was like a government flunky, thought Georgie. An expert at hovering on the very edge but never too far away. In a second Beatrice was off the bed and out the door.

They must have passed each other on the stairs and had the very briefest of exchanges – a quick kiss and fondle? – because Benjamin was up and in her room within seconds.

As he leant over her to kiss her head she could smell, as ever, cardboard packaging and plastic wrapping. It must be all over his skin.

"Beautiful day out there," he said and sat at the foot of the bed. "You all right?"

She didn't want to tell him that she'd been out in the car or about the confrontation with the Youngster.

"Yes, had a walk in the sun, thank you."

"You know you mustn't go close to anyone? You could catch it again."

"I know."

He took out his phone and inspected his messages while she glanced back at her laptop. She saw there was an email from Dr Croft.

"What's this? Something from Mum's doctor."

He looked up briefly.

"Oh yeah?"

Georgie clicked on the email and opened it. There was an attachment and very brief message from Dr Croft.

Dear Mrs Greenfield, please find attached a copy of your mother's death certificate. Once again, my sincerest condolences. With all good wishes, Margaretta Croft.

That stopping again. The freezing.

"Benjamin, it's the death certificate. I forgot all about it."

At once, he was with her, kneeling on the floor so that he could be level with the screen.

"Are you OK to open it? Do you want me to do it, Mum?"

Perhaps it would be good for them if she trusted him with it. It almost took the pain away, to think that she was asking for his help and that he was willing to supply it. She turned the screen to face him and Benjamin read the document through, frowning.

"Tell me," she said.

He chewed his lip and deepened his concentration. He appeared to be reading it over and over.

"Mum…"

"What's the cause of death?"

"The cause of death?" he asked vaguely.

"What else could I be interested in, Benjamin? Please."

She watched his dark eyes skip across the screen.

"The cause of death is given as subdural haematoma."

"What's that?" asked Georgie, searching for her phone, tapping in the words. She grasped at definitions, desperately picked what she needed. "A bleed on the brain. From injury. It's usually from an injury." She looked up at her son. "Oh Benjamin."

But he was already looking at her, aghast.

"Mum, I'm so sorry. It's not…it's not how we think it is. I don't quite understand…"

"What?" she asked. Why did he look so guilty? There was nothing that could hurt her. He should know that. "Tell me what."

"It's this bit here. The bit that describes grandma. It's…"

"It's what, Benjamin?"

"It describes her as…"

"As what? For pity's sake!"

"As the wife of Alan Julian Shattock of 7, Dene Close."

Their mouths were open, their breath caught. They were looking at each other in bewilderment.

"Mum, they were married."

*

It took more than an hour of calling, calling back, waiting, threatening, begging, but at last Dr Croft returned Georgie's call. Benjamin had remained with her as they had waited. At first there had been shocked silence from both of them, then outrage, then disbelief. It's a mistake, they both agreed, over and over again. A misunderstanding by the registrar.

They had no one else to turn to at that moment than the doctor, possibly the last person to have seen Cherry and the Youngster together.

If the doctor had been mindful and zealous in the email, then the sympathy had run out. She clearly felt harassed and had things to say herself.

"Mrs Greenfield, I hear you were very abrupt with the receptionist. I know you're having to process upsetting information, but they're only doing their job. I wonder just how seriously non-medical people are taking this whole situation out there…"

"It's a mistake. There's a mistake on the death certificate," said Georgie. "What do I do about that?"

The voice on the other end of the line paused. When it returned, it was curious.

"What kind of mistake? Maybe you don't quite understand the medical terminology."

"Not that. It says they were married. That's not right."

"Ah."

(If ever an ah carried so much weight.)

"So, they weren't married?" asked Georgie. "Then that's an error."

The doctor's tone was different now. For the first time Georgie heard the vulnerability in it. Perhaps even a sense of remorse.

"I think he did refer to your mother as his wife the last time that I saw them."

"He was lying."

"I don't think you can lie about that kind of thing on a death certificate. It would be picked up."

"But…how? When?"

"When lockdown was suspended, then, as I understand it, registry office marriages resumed."

Georgie felt Benjamin's hand on her arm.

"Listen," said Dr Croft. "I can't really say much more but the truth is I was a little uncomfortable about it myself. I knew that she wasn't really able to make reliable decisions for herself and he seemed so much in control of everything. But I have no reason to think that he had anything but her best interests at heart. And the cause of death is very explicable. Undisputable. It's quite common, I'm afraid, in older patients with dementia. Moments of confusion may lead to a fall and a bump on the head. As we get older our brains reduce in volume, leave a kind of hollow gap under the skull. Even a small bump on the head can cause tearing of tiny blood vessels around a brain. And it would appear that your mother already had a swollen blood vessel. These things often go undiagnosed because the dementia sufferer if already showing the same signs of confusion. And then it's too late. I'm sorry. I'm sorry about all of this piling on top of you. It must be very worrying. She was…loved, you know. Cared for."

Not by me. I wasn't there.

"I may need a statement from you for legal purposes," said Georgie.

"What? No, no. I'm not involved in that way."

But Georgie rang off.

Benjamin was watching her face intently, his hand still clutching her arm.

"They think the whole bloody world has to stop because there's a virus," she said. "*I* won't stop. I won't let him do this to me."

Her son seemed crushed. She wondered at it. Had he given up already, accepted the seeming status quo? No, this wasn't as it seemed. They were meant to give up, let the Youngster live the rest of his life unquestioned. In Cherry's house. Eating at her table, sitting on her sofa, sleeping in her bed.

No. It was unthinkable.

"Don't give up," she said. "He won't win."

21

She slept only briefly, her consciousness returning instantly, like a light going on. Within minutes there was a gentle tap on the bedroom door.

"I heard all the details from Benjamin last night," said Beatrice.

Georgie heaved herself up to sitting.

"I have a lot to get through today. Calls to make. Information to look up."

Beatrice positioned herself, as ever, beside Georgie, pulled the duvet up to her waist.

"Shouldn't you give yourself time to grieve?"

Georgie was irritable.

"Do you think I'm not grieving? I'm grieving all the time. Why do people seem to think otherwise?"

"Oh!" That automatic raising of her hand to her mouth. "I'm so sorry. Of course you are."

"It's all right. I can't really explain it. It's like there's a blackness inside, a hole. I'm peering into it and yet I'm a part of it and it's a part of me. I don't think it'll ever go away." Her voice was breaking and so she coughed and let it settle. "I can grieve *and* get to the bottom of this."

"If anyone can, you can."

Georgie reached down to pick up her laptop from the floor and switched it on.

"He's lying. He made them put husband on the death certificate. They took his word for it. It's not true. How dare he!"

She swivelled the laptop and showed Beatrice the document. Georgie watched as the girl struggled to suppress a smile.

"What's so funny?"

"It's…" A sheepish dropping of her eyes to her lap. "Sorry, it's his name. Shattock. It's got shat in it."

Georgie turned the screen back towards her and spent a good few silent moments looking for contact details for the local marriage registry office. "Wait a minute," she said. "I'm an idiot. Colleen will help."

Beatrice waited for enlightenment.

"I have a neighbour, some doors down, who does this kind of thing, a registrar. Or used to be. Why didn't I think of her before?"

"Yes!" declared her companion, suddenly animated. "That's brilliant. You must go to her right now. You've got to keep pressing on, Georgie. You've mustn't let him win."

*

Colleen Burge listened from her doorstep, neither inviting Georgie in, not coming closer to her than a good metre. She enquired after Georgie's health and reminded her that she could catch it again – or indeed, pass it to someone else. Georgie launched straight into her questions. She didn't wish to talk of her mother and referred to an "elderly friend". Could a person – she asked – claim to be a husband of the deceased without the fact being checked?

"Oh for sure. There's no cross-referencing of these things on a death certificate, but I've never known it to happen. People don't lie about being married. Is it someone round here?"

Georgie pressed on.

"And you wouldn't officiate in a marriage if one party was of unsound mind, would you?"

Colleen smiled at Georgie's formalities. They were the same age and their children had grown up together but they were not close, as such, each grateful for the other's standoffishness.

"Of course not. We take both the bride and groom aside separately and ask them questions."

"What kind of questions?"

"Name and address, how long they've lived at their home, how long they've known each other. We do it because I'm afraid we do get attempts at fraudulent marriages, for visa purposes or..."

"One person taking financial advantage over another, older person?"

"Yes, I'm afraid so. How is Benjamin coping with all this nonsense? He graduated, didn't he? I do feel sorry for them, don't you?"

"He's fine, enjoying working in the real world. But what happens if you think one of the people is being taken advantage of? Do you stop the wedding?"

Georgie's neighbour shifted on the step, glanced behind her.

"We can do, yes. But it's often a difficult call. If two adults are in love and want to get married, then who are we to stop them? Old people fall in love, you know. You'd be surprised."

Georgie's face collapsed into wrinkled distaste.

"Witnesses. They'd need witnesses, right?"

"Of course. Often, they bring a whole group of people to celebrate. Sometimes they just hoik two people out of the waiting room."

"Colleen, can I ask you a huge favour?"

"You do look tired, Georgina. And ever so thin. Are you sure you're all right?"

"Can you find out for me if my mother got married in the past three months?"

*

At the bottom of the garden the sun lingered. It was the last place to catch it before the night arrived. Georgie sat and waited. She was underdressed and occasionally a shiver ran through her. She welcomed the cold, like it was a current bringing her to life.

Old people fall in love.

She pictured Cherry being taken aside and questioned by the registrar.

How long have you known him? Are you sure you want to get married? Do you love him? Do you understand what is happening today?

There were days when Cherry could be lucid, could convince anyone of the clarity of her thinking. Had it been one of those days? She would have reeled off her address and date of birth with no problems. But what would she have said if asked about love? What would anyone say if questioned about their truest feelings? Georgie had never had to field such a question. Her wedding had taken place in a country church because Sam said it would please his parents. She had waited politely for the vicar to stop speaking, kissed her new husband and left the ceremony behind with relief. Funny, but she didn't look back on her own milestones with Sam very much. The past – light or dark – belonged to Cherry.

Was this the furthest reach of agony, then? The real abysmal low of loss? When she saw those people on the news, suffering, having lost loved-ones in war zones or to disease, was this what they felt? Was she allowed, as a comfortable, professional woman in her large suburban house, to find kinship with the victims of a harsher world? There was a masochism to sorrow – she knew it – because if it didn't prevail, then what was left?

Benjamin was coming across the lawn. In the gloom his height seemed accentuated, his dark colourings darker still. When he arrived, only his eyes hinted at sorrow. He was clearly going to try to be hearty.

"Dad not home yet?"

Georgie shook her head.

"He's having to deal with all the flak from the exam results fiasco."

All the lights were off in the house and the stone terrace stood out pale and detached in the distance like a landing stage in a gloomy sea. Benjamin had come home via the side gate, which was always left open for him.

She waited for him to settle and find the right words and tell her the facts of his meeting.

That afternoon Georgie and Benjamin had got to the bottom of Cherry's marital status. Colleen had come over and explained to them what she'd discovered: that a colleague at Bromley Register Office had indeed overseen the marriage of Cherry Weston and Alan Shattock earlier in the summer. Just one unremarkable couple among the many that had put their ceremonies on hold because of the lockdown. There was perhaps a sense of urgency, said Colleen, about actioning these backlogged marriages. And, well, this colleague had something of a reputation, was skating on thin ice because of her suspect decisions in the past.

"Then I'm going to have her investigated," said Georgie. "I'm going to report her."

"Please do," said Colleen. "But first, I advise that you catch up with this Alan Shattock and ask him about the funeral arrangements. I knew of a similar case when the new husband just went ahead and organised a cremation without even telling the rest of the family."

Benjamin had insisted on going to see the Youngster. He thought Shattock might open the door to a stranger and that, once they were face to face, Benjamin could get to the bottom of things. Georgie knew her son was right. And so she sat at the back of the garden and waited for him. The sun had gone down and the chill evening arrived.

*

"He's not very likeable, is he?" Benjamin began.

"Tell me what's happened, please."

Her voice was so small that Benjamin shuffled closer to her on the bench.

"You're cold."

"You're prevaricating."

"I'm not," he said. "Don't worry. I think I've stopped him. He was planning to hold the cremation on Friday, but I've talked him out of it. He's agreed to let us co-organise a funeral."

"There'll be a burial," said Georgie. "I want a grave. I want to visit it. I want to be able to go somewhere and say sorry."

Benjamin sat like a man, thought Georgie, his legs wide open, no space for her. They were strangers to each other, men and women. That was the attraction and the threat.

"I'll help you, Mum. I know which funeral home he's using. He's definitely agreed to let us sit in on the arrangements."

"Can we trust him?"

He turned to her.

"I'll bloody brain him if he lied to me."

You can tell he's a well-brought up young man. That's what Cherry had said. If anything had illustrated her mother's diminished mental acumen, then allowing the Youngster into her life was unquestionably it.

What did Cherry answer, when she was asked by the registrar if she loved him? Was it a hurried yes? Or was it one of those laconic smiles that used to madden her daughter? You could interpret them as you wanted, take away a confirmation if that's what pleased you. But to Georgie, who needed to have answers, they were infuriating and entirely unnecessary.

"What if he's already sorted it all out. What if we're not part of the picture?"

She didn't even know she'd said it out loud, the internal and the external so confused these days.

But when she turned to her son and saw the glistening corners of his eyes, she knew that he was entertaining the same possibilities, reaching his own point of cheerless and unwanted wisdom.

"He's given me his word," said Benjamin, getting up and gesturing for her to rise. As she got up, he placed his arm around her shoulders and pulled her into his chest.

"Let's go in and make a list of who to invite."

22

Annika swept into the house like a cyclone, her voice preceding her, her clothes, scarf, voice swirling around her. She was enormous now, her hair white and short like a pelt above her tanned face. She opened her arms and pressed Georgie against her. Georgie was greeted by huge soft breasts and pungent perfume.

"My heart is broken," she said, stepping back to examine her old friend's daughter. "I must hear everything. But first we must cry together."

In fact, Annika made Georgie smile, not weep. She was a vision in turquoise linen, dressed for a Mediterranean summer, not a damp September morning. Her strong, bare arms were dimpled and an entirely different colour to her face which bordered on brick red. Her eyelids were sky blue and her brows largely and clumsily drawn on. And yet she was such a presence, such a vigorous, stable force, that Georgie kept close to her, like a quivering pet constantly under its owner's feet. It was Annika who led Georgie through the house – despite never having been there – and into the kitchen where they settled at the table. When Georgie offered to make tea or coffee, Annika waved both options away impatiently. Georgie pressed a coffee on her all the same, needing a moment to reset herself after her visitor's emphatic arrival.

"It should not have ended like this."

Everyone else had pussy-footed around her. Annika Walter was unlikely to do anything of the sort. And so Georgie spoke her mind and her heart. She had only given Annika the barest details over the phone. Now she could speak directly and honestly. She could explain what she was feeling and what she wanted. She could be tragic and useless but she could also conspire and damn and rail.

"This bastard man, he's in her house now?"

"Yes, but I'll get him out."

Annika, heartsick, stirred her coffee, shook her head.

"Your poor mother. She was such a clever woman with such a strong mind. Always with the wonderful plans and ideas. She made our business successful. But I liked to talk to her so much, you see. Because I could learn so much. So clever. She used beautiful words."

In the past few days, talking to some of her mother's friends, she learnt what bereaved loved-ones often discover: that their relative was a different person to everyone she met. Georgie had never thought of Cherry as a user of beautiful words, but now that she thought about it, it was patently true.

"And this horrible person, this Youngster, this was not the kind of man she liked."

"I don't think my mother went in for men, did she?"

"Went in for?" asked Annika.

"She didn't have boyfriends."

"Dear God," roared the visitor. "No boyfriends? She had *lots* of boyfriends."

"I don't remember."

"When we ran the business you weren't around, my dear. You had your own life. You didn't know."

Georgie was struggling. Her evident inner conflict softened Annika's approach.

"But none of them was good enough for her. Not one man lasted. It was a bit of fun. She liked their company, that's all. No one was important in that way to her. You, my darling, were the important one. You and your boy. Where is he?"

Georgie got up to stand by the sink and look out into the garden. There was a preponderance of red – salvias and rudbeckias mainly – and a depth of green that presaged brown. The lawn was straggly and still yellow in places, with apples rotting where they'd fallen. She narrowed her eyes and let the colours pour into each other. From behind her, she could hear Annika take a noisy, indulgent mouthful of her coffee. When she turned, she saw her guest grimacing.

"A bit on the strong side for me," she said. "Maybe milk after all."

"Let's go and sit on the terrace," said Georgie.

*

"You could say," said Annika, her biscuit disintegrating in her cup, "that at least our dear Cherry was not alone when so many old people were by themselves and lonely. She had a companion. And you were ill. You could not be with her. I, personally, think this is all rubbish. Madness. Let everyone catch it. We all take risks. Most of us survive. Look at you!"

As ever, one of Annika's speeches contained so many bald statements that Georgie had to pause and choose what to pick up on.

"What kind of companion changes door locks, Annika? What kind of companion won't let a person talk to her daughter on the phone?"

"Ach. Awful man."

"That's what I can't bear, you see. The not knowing what she was going through. Was she frightened? Was she trying to reach out to me and not being allowed to? This is my mother. And she died without me."

It was impossible, at last, to prevent a single tear emerging. At once Georgie's face was enveloped in the soft breasts again, her head held tight in fleshy hands. Above her, Annika was spitting expletives. When Georgie emerged, she felt the sting of a cool breeze on her hot face.

"Have you seen her?" asked Annika.

Georgie lowered her eyes.

"No."

"But you must!"

"I don't want to."

"Rubbish. That's out of the question. Not seeing your mother? How will you say goodbye? How will you accept that she has gone?"

Accept? Georgie thought. Why should I accept?

And then the men were there, Sam and Benjamin arriving on the terrace, all stiff smiles and awkward postures. Hands were shaken, condolences accepted. Annika was full of praise for the height of Cherry's grandson.

The visitor shared some anecdotes of her former business partner with the assembled family and comfortably held court, but she wasn't yet ready to let go of her insistence on this notion of acceptance.

"Tell your mother, darling, that she must go and see Cherry. Say goodbye. I know it's a difficult thing to do but really, she must."

Benjamin looked mutely at his mother and Georgie saw his distress. This issue was too personal and off limits for both of them. But it was Sam who surprised her.

"I think Annika's right," he said. "I think there needs to be an end. A proper end."

"I don't know…" Georgie broke off, imagining her mother once more as the medieval tomb effigy, refusing to picture flesh, closed eyes, sunken cheeks.

Sam reached across the garden table and picked up her hand.

"I can come with you."

"It's…it's not that."

"Then what, Geeny? Should Benjamin be with you? I don't mind."

Georgie looked at all the faces around the table, their concern, their obvious disquiet.

"I suppose I'm scared."

Nods and murmurs. Of course, of course.

"No, you don't understand. I'm scared that I might realise something, see in her a rebuke of some sort. She might have changed, he might have changed her, and then she wouldn't be mine anymore. I don't know if she's still mine…"

Sam's hand suddenly constricted. It was how he communicated these days.

"She's yours. Geeny, she's yours. And you are hers. Nothing changed."

"Yes! Something changed. She relied on him. He was the only one with her. Not one of you seemed to care. You just thought it convenient."

She wasn't a child. Leaving in a tearful rush was not acceptable behaviour though this would be the perfect moment. She readied herself for departure.

"That's not fair, Mum," said Benjamin.

At once her morale collapsed. Look at him! He was so unhappy and not just for her, but for himself. He had lost his grandmother. And Sam...so helpless, so incapable of saying the right thing. How far apart they had moved since her illness. A great wedge had been driven between them because of her inability to explain and confide. But it might be too late. Should she just please them? Were they even right? She glanced now at Annika, their unperturbable visitor – even she was knocked by the depth of Georgie's grief. Even she had come to a standstill.

"All right. All right," muttered Georgie. "I'll go."

It won't end anything. But I'll go.

*

Two exchanges from that morning remained with her when she went to bed that night.

As she had led Annika down the front path to her car, she had suddenly exclaimed: "Oh Annika! There's someone I want you to meet. Benjamin's girlfriend. Where on earth is she?" And as she had been looking around, glancing at the upstairs windows, it had occurred to her that Beatrice's appearances and absences were not at all random but entirely strategic. As though the girl was choreographing moments between Georgie and her family.

"She would have to be pretty special for that perfect boy," said Annika, climbing breathily into her tiny car.

"She is," said Georgie. "Though a little strange, I think. But wonderful in her way!"

And then, tonight, just as she had emerged from her bathroom, Sam had been there waiting.

"Is it time, do you think?" he asked.

"What for?" She walked past him, climbed into her bed.

"For you to come back to our bedroom. Our bed. I can't help thinking you shouldn't be alone so much."

She didn't know. She hadn't thought about it. Was she alone? Was that a problem?

"Would you like me to come with you tomorrow?" he asked, hovering over her. "To the funeral home? Do you want me to make an appointment for you?"

"Are we meant to make appointments?"

"I don't know."

She remembered how he had been at that tense gathering in the garden earlier. Always a fish out of water, Sam Greenfield, when it came to social engagements. His job was to wait and watch and to arrive with the right answers. That's how advisers worked. It was never her forte. She had always put her head down and worked alone, presenting the fruits of that labour to the next layer of bureaucracy. Sam needed confirmation that he was of use, saying the right things. Georgie needed to be trusted, secure that she was right.

"Soon," she told him. "I'll come back soon."

Which, he knew, meant that it was time for him to leave her room.

23

She saw him as she walked up the high street towards the funeral home.

He was up ahead, loitering in front of the chemist's shop. He was in a black leather biker jacket which was a little too large for him, his fingertips poking from beneath the cuffs. It was evidently new, the arms comically stiff and held away from his sides. He was in his usual aviators and jeans.

"Cunt," said Georgie under her breath and put her head down so that he wouldn't see her.

She would deal with him soon enough but now wasn't the time. She wanted this moment to be pure and memorable. Perhaps it was already sullied, just by the sight of him.

Beatrice had declined to come with her, even though she was the only one that Georgie invited. The girl had actually physically backed off at the idea.

"I'm so sorry but I don't think I'd be able to do that."

The polite refusal didn't come as much of a surprise.

"Do I involve you in too much, Beatrice? Am I dragging you around and making you fed up with me?"

The girl's expression had been sweet, so natural and honest. She was – it felt to Georgie – an embodiment of human spirit, responding to each challenge with a moral measure. It seemed to come naturally to her. She was – somehow – Georgie's reverse, her negative. An instinctively good person but with all the concomitant softness, even-handedness and vacillation. Together they were as effective as a human could be. Alone, they were often a little lost with how to deal with other people.

And so Georgie slipped out of the house without anyone else noticing, having sworn Beatrice to play dumb if anyone asked about her whereabouts. She took the long way down to the town, avoiding the estate and Cherry's house, skirting the park rather than going through it and seeing their bench.

The Youngster entered the pharmacy and Georgie hurried past and up to the end of town, where the funeral home was based in a Georgian townhouse with a glass annex to the side. *Cattermole Brothers, Family Funerals*, it said, and Georgie pictured an entire group – parents and children – laid to rest in a mausoleum. For years she'd passed the building and never thought twice about it, considering it as tempting fate to even speculate about that kind of business. But now that she was entering the foyer, with its pale blue walls and picked-out white cornicing, she wondered why it had seemed so forbidding. There was a clean and welcoming air in the reception area, with white carnations in a vase on the front desk. A woman in a blue blazer appeared almost as soon as Georgie entered. She'd come from a glass-walled office, where another woman – dressed the same way – still sat at work.

"May I help?" Her name badge said *Joy*.

Somewhere behind that glass office, in a room specifically set aside for the purpose, lay Cherry. In a coffin? Presumably. Georgie had never been in this situation before and didn't know the procedure. But now she was here, she felt emboldened and, surprisingly, business-like. Maybe it was seeing women in suits that so reassured her.

"Yes, I'd like to set about organising a funeral."

Joy's head tilted, and her expression – above her face mask – became tragic.

"Oh dear. I'm sorry for your loss. A close relative?"

"My mother."

"Oh dear, oh dear. Our deepest condolences."

Georgie eyed the woman, perplexed. Surely, these people weren't genuinely moved. Death meant business. There was no need to pretend. And yet – just as it had been when she was in hospital – Georgie found herself deeply grateful for receiving the ritual facial ticks and sound effects. Joy's voice was set at a level of cheerful distress.

"Then shall we make an appointment so that we talk everything through at a time that's convenient to you? We suggest you set aside an hour and a half to make sure that all the details are sufficiently covered."

"We can't do it now?" asked Georgie.

"Oh, no. I'm so sorry. There are procedures. And we're fully booked."

"Could I then, at least, see her? She's here. My mother. Somewhere. Cheryl Weston."

Joy remained silent as she assessed her new client. A stoniness was making itself more apparent. Just as well, thought Georgie. These people needed backbone.

"Mrs Weston?"

"Sorry. She recently re-married. Mrs Cheryl Shattock." Gorgie flinched at the awfulness of the name.

Joy's eyes narrowed.

"Would you give me a moment?"

She was back in the glass office in seconds, leaning over her colleague. Both women had their heads bowed as they spoke, although Joy occasionally flicked her eyes towards Georgie. When they emerged, it was to lead Georgie into yet another office, this time to the side of the reception desk. The two funeral staff waited for Georgie to sit before they settled opposite her across a shiny pine table. Georgie noted the new name badge: *Margaret*.

You're there, somewhere, she thought. For a moment, her mood surged with elation at the idea of seeing Cherry's face again. Now there was no sense of coldness, of the medieval lady in the chapel, but of soft pink skin. Had they put Cherry's signature eyeliner on properly? Would she be allowed to help? That idiot would have had no idea about such things.

"We've never been in this situation before," said the one called Margaret. Joy nodded to emphasise the novelty.

"What situation?"

"She's definitely your mother?"

"Cherry Weston? I mean, Shattock. Yes, definitely. I'm her only daughter. Georgina Greenfield. We live very close to each other. Lived. Everything's happened very quickly. I was ill."

"He...he never said there was a daughter," Margaret looked to Joy. "We got the impression that Mrs Shattock had no children. In fact, no living relatives at all."

"She has plenty of living relatives. Me. Her grandson. And an awful lot of concerned friends. But I'll take care of all that. I know who to invite. We've agreed it with Mr Shattock. It's in my hands now."

Joy this time: "We have forms that have to be filled in. They're the normal procedure. We asked him to fill one in."

Margaret continued for her colleague: "There's a question. It's says: *have all family members been notified of the deceased's passing?*"

From Georgie: "Of course."

"And then it asks: *are all family members aware of the funeral arrangements?*"

"I don't understand."

Georgie looked from one face to another. Two women, probably a little older than her, tired-seeming, as came with the age, a little spent, a little worn.

Joy seemed to be wiping her palms on the sides of her skirt. In preparation for what?

"I thought I had to make an appointment to arrange everything?" said Georgie, watching Joy's elbows move up and down. She was conscious of looking fierce. She knew – Sam often told her – that when people were confusing her, she came across as murderous.

Joy placed a dry hand on the table.

"Well, it's never actually happened that someone has mis-led us like this."

The hand was creeping across the tabletop towards Georgie.

"You see, your mother was cremated yesterday morning. A very small service. I think only Mr Shattock was in attendance. People don't lie about this kind of thing. It's never happened before, has it, Margaret?"

"No," said Margaret, dismally. "Why would anyone fib about telling relatives?"

"And he very definitely didn't want an announcement going into the local paper," came Joy. "Was very adamant about that. It's part of our service, you see. *You* draft the announcement and *we* make sure it goes in the paper. People like a little something to snip out and keep. And you'd be surprised how many mourners show up having read about it in the paper. But…"

"But…" finished Margaret. "He didn't want any of that. Said it was only him. She didn't have anyone else. I mean, we only have a client's word. Why would they fib?"

Joy, with not an iota left in reserve, reached across the table to take Georgie's hand. Georgie focused on the long, lank fingers and the thin silver chain at the wrist. She balled up her own hands and pushed them against herself. Why did they think she would want to touch them?

"I…I wanted to see her. I wanted to speak to her."

"Oh dear. Oh dear, oh dear. This is just awful."

"She's gone."

The two undertakers exchanged glances and seemed to close down spontaneously. Nothing more to say. To apologise might be to admit to liability. They proffered pained expressions.

Georgie's voice, when it came after a few seconds, was so slight that neither woman heard her from the other side of the table.

"My Mama. Forgive me."

24

The world was on the verge of locking down again. Lives would be reducing. Rooms sanctuaries again, or cells. Rules seemed impossible to remember. How many people and where? Inside? Outside? How to breathe. How to talk. Face away, open a window, cover up. Come home and wash your hands at once.

For some it was a common purpose, a moment of ordinary heroism. For some, tedium. And for some others, an outrage. We are not as one but let them tell it as though we are.

Fear was giving way to impatience. Perhaps, you never know, we might escape unscathed and then what will have come of this for the individual? Too much time to think. Too much of the self, full stop. That can't be a good thing, can it?

*

For Georgie, incarceration was more of the same. But it brought with it new frustrations. Where once she would have sought a meeting with a solicitor or a doctor, now she found herself pushed back and told that things were not as normal, that she'd have to be patient. In the meantime, he was slipping away from her and seemed to be thriving.

"What's the point of talking to anyone anyway," Beatrice pointed out. "Who's on your side? Not the police or lawyers. Not even your family can do anything. They want you happy again. But they don't want a fight. They're terrified. I can see it in them. Please let this mess go away, they're thinking. But that's not how you feel. You won't rest over this. It's got to end. It's got to end because you'll be ill again if it doesn't."

Georgie listened and examined the hate within her. It was meant to be a sign of weakness, this degree of animosity. It meant you were on the backfoot, that you were scared for yourself. It wasn't rational. It never ended well. That's what the psychologists said.

"When we found that little house, my mother was ecstatic. She saw so much promise. I didn't. I thought it was ugly and beneath her. But you know, she made something beautiful out of it. She could transform the least promising things. It became a part of her. And she once told me that, when the time came, when she reached the end, she could think of nothing better than being in her pretty little bedroom on a sunny morning, me beside her holding her hand, the birds singing. Springtime, probably."

"What if he sells it?" asked the girl.

"I *want* him to sell it! I don't want him in it a moment longer. Let someone else have it and love it. But not him. He's polluting it. And I want her things. That's the start. I'll get them back. Her garden, Bea...all the things we planted together. I'm prepared to dig it all up, if that's what it takes. He's not allowed anything that she touched or loved or made."

And they agreed that, while they were still free to be out and not yet locked up at home, Georgie should emerge once again and be cool with the Youngster and play on any iota of sympathy he might have for a bereaved daughter. Any little victory would be welcome.

*

He was in the black biker jacket. It was so new that it refused to move with his body, the leather stiff and ungiving. When he lifted the mug, a huge crease formed at the elbow and he could barely get it to his lips.

The Youngster was in Frank's, the very same café where Georgie and Cherry had often ended up after their walks. The weather had finally and conclusively turned after a summer of seemingly endless heat and brightness. On TV, the weather presenters talked of autumn as though it were a curse coming down on a blighted people. Georgie barely even noticed the weather and the changing seasons, but Beatrice had suggested she might want to order something warmer than the linen dress. They picked out a new outfit for her: a black jersey shirt, some brown cords and a deep red boiled wool cardigan that would also serve as a jacket. When Sam had seen her in the cardigan his eyes had lit up. "You look great," he said. "You should wear more strong colours like that."

Beatrice's only concession to the cooler weather was a navy blue hoody. Georgie thought it looked familiar, might be Benjamin's. She had been wearing it as they both delivered a letter to Cherry's house the day before. Georgie had said she wanted the Youngster to know how she felt about the cremation. Nothing too emotional, nothing threatening. Only the fact that he had done her a terrible wrong by misleading her. She wanted it written down. She wanted him to pause over the words and contemplate the effect of his actions. But most of all, she wanted him to know that he wasn't dealing with an idiot or a pushover.

And now here he was, sitting alone and encased in his new jacket, his mug on the tabletop beside a plate bearing a half-consumed slice of carrot cake. He was looking straight head of him at the opposite wall.

Georgie and Beatrice hovered on the pavement outside. The café had a sign up saying only five customers were allowed in at any one time. In fact, people were steering clear of public places and, if there was a queue, Georgie and Beatrice were it.

"This is *my* place," said Georgie. "This is where we came together. Why is *he* here?"

"You're not going to go in, are you?" asked Beatrice with evident anxiety.

"Why not?"

"I won't join you."

"I didn't think you would."

Georgie pushed the door open and stepped inside the café. The last time she'd been there was with Cherry, more than half a year ago, such a commonplace visit that the details of their conversation had long faded. At least he wasn't at their usual table. He was lifting the cake to his mouth when Georgie pulled a chair back and sat down opposite him.

She half expected him to get up and leave but he surprised her by continuing to eat with every semblance of calm. As he raised the mug to his lips, she heard the crunch of new leather.

"I saw you outside," he said. "Are you following me again?" He produced a phone from his pocket and laid it on the table. "I'll call the police."

"I want her things."

He looked down at his sleeve and removed a crumb. "What things?"

"*Her* things, her personal effects. You don't need them."

"Yes, but what things exactly?"

The Youngster's face and neck had a crumbling texture, some flakes of dry skin balancing on his stubble. His hands, however, were smooth and unmarked, his fingernails clean and uniformly shaped. She found them wrong, like they'd been taken from a child and attached to his wrists.

"Photographs, clothes, letters to me. Gifts I gave her. Her jewellery, some of the pictures on the walls."

"Photographs?" he said and though she'd heard his diluted Scottish accent before, she only properly placed it now. "I don't know of any photographs."

"I know where she kept them. I could come in and remove them. That's all. I can be quick. In and out."

A lop-sided smile and a supercilious shake of the head. "Jewellery? I don't think so. Some of it's quite valuable."

He was accusing her of something but she wasn't at all sure of what. Cherry didn't have valuable jewellery. It was a nonsense, a new insult, to suggest that Georgie was trying to scrape together some kind of financial gain from the loss of her mother. She turned and peered through the café window to see Beatrice but there was no sign of her.

"These things mean a lot to me. It was always understood that I would have them. It's in the will, for God's sake."

"Ah," he said and stretched his arms to the side, the leather sighing and creaking. "A new marriage automatically revokes a will, I think you'll find. Look it up. It's all mine now. In my keeping. And I want it all together and under one roof."

"Why?" she demanded, sitting forward. He moved back with a nervous jerk.

"Because it's what she'd want."

Georgie leant in closer.

"Don't you tell me what she'd fucking want."

He tried to fold his arms but the unsupple leather wasn't having it.

"Please leave."

"I want her things."

"Sorry." And he looked away.

What could she do? Remain where she was until she forced him to change his mind? Threaten him?

"Then I'll get my lawyer to formally ask for them. You'll have to hand them over. It's a reasonable request."

"I'll destroy them first."

It was delivered quietly and as lightly as a punchline.

"What?"

The Youngster got up.

"I'm leaving. Goodbye."

Georgie was still sitting, stunned. "I don't understand. They're photographs of my life with my mother. They're precious. You can't want them or need them."

He looked down at her as though she were a beggar and his patience and goodwill had run out.

"You don't deserve them," he said and pushed his way past the empty chairs to leave the café and her behind.

Georgie got up at once, her head swimming. She followed him out of the café and dogged him along the pavement. Whenever he looked back at her, there was a barely-concealed almost theatrical terror in his eyes.

You wet bastard, she was thinking. *You're all talk. It would be so easy to hurt you.*

She got up behind him, called out to him. "What the hell do you mean I don't deserve them?"

He was trotting now. Every now and again he skipped off the kerb to give the few other pedestrians a melodramatically wide berth. She had no choice but to follow this lunatic dance.

They were heading away from the high street and from the estate and Cherry's house. Georgie had hoped that she could trail him back to the house and somehow convince him to let her in. But he was determined to go another way. She had no choice now but to stick with him or lose face. But as they continued, she began to wonder how it should end? Should she tell him that she'd spoken to the same police officer who this time seemed more alert to the Youngster's questionable behaviour? Could she threaten him with the law, bamboozle him with a few choice terms that would be meaningless but sufficiently intimidating?

He stopped so abruptly that she almost ran into him and when he turned around, she saw rage.

"What? Are you going to follow me all the way to Halfords?"

Cars were passing them at speed and she wasn't sure if she'd caught every word.

"Halfords?" she asked.

The Youngster was suddenly delighted.

"I'm picking up my helmet for my new motorbike. *Buy yourself a new bike, Alan,* she said. *If it makes you happy.* She was so keen to make me happy. So that's what I've done. You can come with me to see the helmet if you want. I can't think why you would."

There was so much processing to do and Georgie always needed time. The Youngster was moving off. She grabbed his arm, her fingers slipping on the new leather. He pulled away with disgust.

"I just want her things." She surprised herself that she was pleading. "You don't need them. You'd probably want to be shot of them."

"And then?" he asked.

"What do you mean *then*?"

"You want everything, young lady."

"What the fuck?"

She stepped backwards in her confusion, one of her feet sliding off the kerb. The Youngster was staring her down. *Young lady?* Who on earth did he think he was!

"Shall I tell you why you don't deserve Cheryl's things?"

The cars pounded by, her hearing was patchy, she couldn't keep up. What should she do?

"I'll tell you," he said, moving a step closer, making sure she didn't miss a word. His features were contorted, overemphatic, the mouth ridged with distaste. And still all she looked at were the flakes of dry skin around his neck and shoulders. A single one detached itself and flew off into the traffic. "Because I found her that day. She was sitting on the bench alone. No coat on. Just slippers. On a winter's day! She was crying. No one to look after her. A virus everywhere and her so vulnerable. Totally alone. She didn't even know where she lived. How could anyone do that? Leave that wonderful lady to fend for herself, in her state? It would have to be someone heartless. Someone who just wants her things."

She was seeing Cherry as he must have seen her, shivering, baffled as to why, waiting, not knowing who or what she was waiting for. He found her and, cursing the world that abandoned her, took her back to her house and gave her tea and cheered her up and established himself almost instantly. The new other.

"I was there for her always," he said. "Fed her, dressed her, kept my eye on her. And you know what? I doubt she even remembered she had a daughter. All she had was me and she loved me for it."

"I don't believe you. She wouldn't forget me."

"Her things are very precious to me. They are all I have of her. I won't be parting with them, thank you very much."

When he turned away from her it was decisive. There would be no more following. He moved fast, ducked past a young couple coming in the other direction.

Don't cry. Don't cry.

The autumnal air was so sharp and irritating, pushed her and prodded her, didn't want her standing around. But she couldn't move away.

"She didn't even know who I was."

"That's bollocks," said Beatrice, suddenly there.

"You heard?"

"Just the last bits. He looked very threatening so I came over. Awful, ugly man. I hate him."

"He found her in the park all alone and confused. He was there for her when I wasn't."

"That's what he says." Beatrice was gently ushering Georgie back towards the high street and home. "That's what I'd say if I wanted you off my back. I'd make you feel really bad."

It was past four and the light was thinning into evening.

"It must be true."

"Why?"

Georgie's thoughts trailed off back to Cherry's profile through the windows, the last time she had seen her. She didn't get up to open the door. She was incapable, clutching at anyone – anyone's love.

"I wasn't there."

Everyone, it seemed, was staring at her as she walked past. Beatrice was up ahead. Maybe they thought she was talking to herself, a teary madwoman, possibly unstable. Was this just a fraction of the distress and desolation that Cherry had felt sitting alone on the bench, the world locked-up, her daughter rapidly disappearing from what was left of her precious memory? Should she be grateful to the near-stranger who came by and had the wit and sympathy to check on her and see what was wrong?

But why did it have to be him? A conceited bastard who clearly now felt that the world was finally turning his own way and that no one could turn it back in the other direction.

25

They were in the garden of Red Door House. Cherry was cutting back a fatsia to make room for something new, Georgie hadn't caught what. It was a warm Saturday morning in April and Georgie had strolled over from The Brake and caught her mother just changing into her gardening clothes. She sat at the little cast iron table while Cherry worked.

"It's parents' evening next week. Are you coming?"

Her mother stopped and the secateurs landed back at her side. She was in jeans and a man's striped shirt that she'd bought at a charity shop specifically for housework.

"Are you sure you want me there again?" she asked, turning around to look at Georgie.

"I most definitely do. It's the last one before his GCSEs. It's very important."

"No, I mean, are you sure you want *me* there? Won't Sam want to go?"

Georgie inspected the top of the table as she spoke.

"He doesn't know. I don't like to bore him with domestic minutiae."

"Georgie girl!" Cherry came and stood in front of the table and waved her secateurs in the air. "Of course he's going to want to know about this. Doesn't he ever ask why I've attended school events and not him?"

Georgie was eyeing the secateurs with distaste.

"I don't bother him with it. He's got enough on his plate without listening to teachers about grade predictions. But if you don't want to go."

Her mother sat down on the other iron chair.

"I'd love to go, darling. You know that. I always have. But it's struck me recently that you seem a little, well, a little scared of Sam sometimes."

"What!" Those tiny embers of teenage resentment glowed suddenly. Georgie felt sick with the memory of past squabbles. She didn't want to recall them. "I'm not scared of Sam. What a thing to level at me."

"I don't mean you think he's going to slap you or anything. I mean, you treat him like he's fragile. That the slightest demand might make him shatter into pieces."

"Oh Mum."

"No, really. Why do you think he wouldn't want to be involved in his son's school events? He's your husband. Benjamin's father."

"Don't sound so Victorian."

Cherry shrugged and got up and returned to the fatsia.

"I can't believe *you're* giving *me* marriage advice," said Georgie sullenly. "Sam and I have been together nineteen years. We must have got something right."

Cherry was pushing back a branch with her shoulder so that she could reach into the heart of the bush. "There's more to marriage than simply staying together, isn't there?"

"How on earth would you know? There's nothing wrong with Sam and me."

"There's nothing wrong with *Sam*."

"Mum!"

Cherry had turned around to look at her daughter with that placatory smile, all tenderness and pity, which should have pushed her daughter further into indignation, but had instead reduced her to troubled silence. They wouldn't fight. They never fought these days. Cherry wasn't mischievous anymore. Her loyalties were with her daughter, Georgie knew that. If she was moved to make a comment, then she would have given it plenty of thought beforehand. Georgie wouldn't let herself be angry, held back from the worst of her thoughts, but sometimes, when they parted, she wanted to scream. Could it be that her mother was right about everything and always? Did that come with age? What did she see that Georgie couldn't?

Yes, she divined everything sooner or later. That's why Georgie kept so much from her.

*

Georgie sat up in bed and leant forward, her head dropped to her chest. At the point of waking, she'd been crying. As though her dream ordained it. She didn't remember the dream, only had the tears to guide her.

"Why did you marry him?" she demanded from the darkness. "You stupid fucking bitch! Why? Why would you go and marry him?"

*

"It's just such a pity that your mother married him," said PC Hitchin. "That's the problem you're facing."

"I know," said Georgie curtly.

"If he'd just moved in, we'd have him. He wouldn't have a leg to stand on. We'd just go to court and get him out of there."

"Yes, I realise that."

The policewoman was talking from a busy office. Georgie could hear laughter and the tapping of keyboards. Leah Hitchin had given Georgie her direct number but Georgie hadn't been moved to use it until now.

"He had her cremated."

"Well within his rights, as the spouse."

"But he didn't tell any of us. I wasn't at my own mother's funeral."

"That's very sad, Mrs Greenfield."

"And now he won't let me have any of her things."

"They're technically his things. That's the problem."

In the background, someone was offering to buy a round of teas. Georgie hadn't been in an office for so long that she suddenly felt a pang of nostalgia.

"Why didn't you go for one of them power of attorney things?"

"I didn't have a chance. My mother was diagnosed and deteriorated very quickly. I was…I was out of things for a long time. Somehow, he managed to convince the registrar that they loved each other."

"Is it possible?" asked the policewoman.

Georgie had to quell the rising indignation. "No, it's not possible that they loved each other. That's what the solicitor asked. She brought up the issue of the Lasting Power of Attorney as well."

"And?"

"And I told her what I've just told you. I didn't know she was going to spiral downwards so quickly. I didn't know I was going to catch a virus and get very ill. I didn't know that a stranger would step into the vacuum. I didn't know any of this beforehand. How could I?"

The police officer remained silent while the room behind her buzzed and reverberated with calls and cackles.

"Couldn't you call on him?" pushed Georgie. "As a community officer. Ask him to give me my mother's belongings? The solicitor wrote to him but, the thing is, he knows where he stands. He's got a lawyer of his own."

"I bet he has. There's always a solicitor hovering somewhere."

She had to let it pass. All her working life she'd bitten her lip over such comments about the supposed venality of her profession. But then she was as distanced from the high street practitioner as it was possible for a fellow lawyer to be. Was she even a lawyer anymore? When she had worked, there had been something fertile about it, words begetting words, worlds building more worlds. Dealing with people's complaints was the last thing she would have contemplated doing.

"I'll do it," said Leah.

"You'll call on him?"

"I don't have no power to enter the property - let's get that straight - and I can't accuse him of anything or question him. I'll just say that I'm dealing with the concerned enquiries of another party. If he closes the door on me, then there's nothing I can do about that. You got that?"

"I just want the photographs. The ones of her and me. That's all."

"I'll ask."

"Thank you," said Georgie. "I won't lie, I feel a bit helpless. Not a nice feeling."

"I don't like the sound of him," said the policewoman. "I wish we'd got there sooner."

*

"Have you been sitting out in the garden?" asked Sam. "In this weather?"

She had entered the kitchen from the outside just as he was arriving from the hall. It was dark and she had to squint to see him under the light.

"It's not cold."

"It *is* cold."

How awkward it suddenly felt, the two of them alone together, the kitchen table between them. Shy? In front of Sam? How on earth did that happen? Maybe because he was inspecting her so closely. It made her uncomfortable.

"You always feel the cold more than I do," she said. "How was work?"

"I'm not going back in the morning. I've said I'll be working from home again." He sat down heavily at the table. She didn't move, watched him.

"What do you mean?"

"They're playing fast and loose. We shouldn't be attending parties. It'll come back to bite us. We're meant to be leading by example."

"Parties?" she asked vaguely. "Who's having parties?"

At last, the merest of smiles from her husband. "Do you remember how we used to drive around on summer evenings? Before Benjamin was born. Before we found The Brake?"

Georgie was nervous of his incipient emotions. She didn't want her train of thoughts diverted.

"Things were simpler."

"They probably weren't. They just seemed that way. And we were younger." He was looking straight ahead of him, his arms seemed collapsed on the table. "I'm tired," he said simply.

She knew what it was. It had been in her bones too, before she had left work. It was impossible for a person to keep this up, to trot after his political masters with an even mood, always armed with answers. They wouldn't accept a void, or so much as a hint of doubt. They couldn't function without their advisers functioning. The stress on her husband, particularly at this time, must have been monumental. When they were young, nothing could disturb their equanimity. They relished work and talked about it when they were home, reluctant to let go of the rushing feeling of being needed. Fatigue was physical and simply wiped out with a good night's sleep.

Now? Now she yearned for the energy of those days, the clarity of her mind then. Nowadays – perhaps spooked by her own mother's mental decline – she was forever in a panic when she forgot something or put the bread in the fridge and the cheese in the breadbin. Not laughable, not comical forgetfulness. A backsliding, a struggle to know oneself. This can't be me, this can't be my mind, this deliquescence. No, not melting, but evaporating into nothing. Is it the end then? The long run to the end?

She could tell him, now, about her fears for the future, of what she might become. Or better still, she could listen, gather him in and let him pour it out to her. They might be struggling together and not even know.

But even as she thought it other thoughts were pushing through, aggressive ones, ones that needed to be heard and considered. The Youngster…what had he said? That he met Cherry in the park, in her nightie, confused, in her slippers, not knowing where she lived. Why had she gone there? She knew not to go out without

Georgie by her side. How come it was the Youngster who had found her and not anyone else? She must have attracted attention. Was he always there, waiting? And what happened once he'd got her home? Did she ask him to stay...stay with her forever? Had they talked about her, about Georgie, and come to the conclusion that she couldn't be relied on, that it was time to leave her behind?

Sam was watching her, his mouth slightly open, his eyes full of wonder. Her face must have been quite something.

"What's wrong?" he said.

How long could Sam wait for her? How much patience can a worn-out man have? How desperately lonely he must be, she suddenly realised. And how incapable she was, just then, to do anything about it. He had to wait for her to come back to him; and if he couldn't, then that was his problem, not hers. She had enough problems of her own and limited time in which to eradicate them.

26

Just before she set off, she called Annika.

She could hear Sam, ensconced back in his office bedroom, in what sounded like a typically heated discussion with a colleague. His raised voice would camouflage her own thoughts and feelings when she talked to Annika. Benjamin was out and, as Beatrice was also nowhere to be seen, Georgie assumed they were somewhere together. The weather was fine for early October and so perhaps they'd gone for a walk. What else was there to do for young people? No one stuck by the half hour rule any more and a trip to the supermarket, despite the queuing and the mask-wearing, was a keenly-anticipated excursion.

Annika listened intently to her plans. Georgie explained that the police officer, PC Hitchin, had called early in the morning to say that yesterday evening Mr Shattock had agreed to hand over a few items at eleven this morning. She was to call round and he would hand things through the door. It was a minor triumph and Georgie needed to tell Beatrice about it, but in the girl's absence, her mother's oldest friend would have to do.

Annika did not respond quite how Georgie had expected.

"You must buy many tins of mackerel."

"I'm sorry?"

"It is very good for the brain. It will help your brain recover. After everything it has been through, the poor thing."

Georgie tried to assimilate the information.

"Thank you. My brain is fine though."

"Your family worries for it. I could tell when I came to visit. They think it is damaged."

Georgie was laughing. Annika must be joking.

"They felt my brain was damaged?"

"I could see how worried they were. But, my dear Georgie girl, it's not your fault. You were very, very ill. You were put to sleep. That kind of thing messes with you. And life is very stressful now."

Georgie girl. How could she? No one else ever called her that.

"I need to go," she told Annika.

"Already?"

"I have to go and buy mackerel."

When she put the phone down she thought: *I never liked you.*

*

The estate was silent. Only a thin string of smoke – someone's autumn bonfire – could be seen dissipating against the vibrant blue of the sky. The layout of the streets was a series of four large squares, with identical low houses looking into paved or grassed centres. Cherry's square was the only one without grass but with tarmacked parking spaces instead, and with a row of white lock-up garages along one side. Not the most prepossessing view outside one's door but it was always neat and there was never any fly-tipping. In fact, Cherry's square was perhaps the best-kept, with a lot of her neighbours the elderly hangers-on from the days when they first bought their council homes back in the 80s.

As Georgie entered her mother's square, a large shopping bag hanging from her left hand, her eyes fell on the usual quaint sights. In front of a couple of homes were miniature plastic picket fences, guarding clumps of begonias and geraniums still going strong in the tired bare soil. Either side of one house were two urns – also plastic – containing imitation ferns, weathered to grey green, their joints very visible between the fronds. It usually made Georgie queasy, to see artificial plants used so prominently, but this time she was almost heartened by them, appreciating their role as emblems of effort. What would Sam make of all this? Of the paucity of beauty or good taste? For the first time in a while she felt lightened, enjoyed discovering the innate comicality of the world, the little gestures that everyone thought made them stand out but which simply shoved them closer to the rest of the pack.

Up ahead was the red door. Her heart struggled, then, because it was still Cherry's door, the door through which they had carried her furniture and the plants for the redesigned back garden. In fact, she remembered the day Cherry had painted it, with Georgie standing by and watching while twittering about her son and her husband, about work colleagues, mesmerised by the up and down of the brush, the lines of red being laid down over the stripped and prepared wood. It had struck her forcefully then how differently they lived, Georgie in her large, sunny, peaceful, detached and lawn-wrapped house, with its wood panelling and French windows; her mother, nearby, in a utilitarian little tub of a place, apparently jerry built, simple to the point of irrelevance. But it was what Cherry wanted and the process of transforming it enlivened her and tested her already considerable powers of improvement and invention.

"Oh, I love a project," Cherry had exclaimed when the sale was completed. "It needs a little love, Georgie girl, that's all. I'd do them all up on the estate if I was allowed. Anyway, it's got perfectly good bones, this sweet little place. We can do a make-over."

Georgie had been less convinced of the quality of the building's bones at first, but grew to realise – as her mother must have done much sooner – that it was the cheapness of the fittings, rather than the main structure, that made it look so flimsy. Cherry found these wounds nothing more than points of interest, to be healed and forgotten. She had filled Georgie in on each one.

"Look! The windows don't fit properly," she pointed out, shortly after moving in. "And one of the doors has been hung the wrong way, would you believe? And the letter box is a mantrap, its sides are so sharp. And the edging on the path is cinder blocks. All sticky-up and getting in the way. They'll have to go first."

Cherry believed in achievement by inspiration. If she felt most moved to renovate the garden, then that's where she would begin. It meant pulling up around five square metres of cement paving and the weeds growing abundantly between them, taking apart a rickety shed and similar fencing and smashing up the narrow concrete patio. Georgie wanted to be involved right from the start, knowing that her mother, who didn't like to waste money by paying other people to do jobs she could do perfectly well herself, couldn't possibly manage alone. Working together, laughing together… how could she have possibly known that those blissful days renovating Cherry's house would one day bring Georgie such painful stabs of yearning? This little house and the exquisite garden beyond were saturated with the joy of the two women who found the most perfect pleasure in working together. It was Cherry's house. Without Cherry it would be nothing to look at, let alone admire.

A black bin was out, waiting on the kerb in front of the house. The collection wasn't until the following day but clearly the Youngster was fastidious. No one else had put their bins out yet. Georgie looked up to the spare bedroom window, expecting to see his face disappear. The breeze brought the bonfire smell to her nostrils. It made her chest tighten and her breathing labour a little. She reached out and knocked on the door and stepped back again. She checked her watch. A minute past eleven. Perhaps he hadn't expected her to be this punctual. She could wait.

From a distant corner of the estate a baby was crying. Georgie's maternal ear settled on the sound. Her heart went out to the child's mother.

She knocked again.

"He said eleven," she told the air.

Would she have to rouse Enid again? Please God, no. She was geared up for one conversation, not two. She had prepared for it, had planned with lawyerly forethought what words she should and could use and what confession she could cleverly wring out of him. She had her phone at hand, in case anything needed recording. She was wound tight, ready. But nobody came to the door. Twice more she knocked and waited, a sickness radiating in her stomach, a premonition.

Then, on cue, Enid opened her door and Georgie's heart sank.

"He won't hear you. He's in the garden."

"Can you tell him I'm here, please?"

Enid's face disappeared from the crack in the door and once again Georgie waited and forced her mind to blankness in preparation. Once the pictures were in her hand, she could go. Maybe tell him what else she wanted but otherwise not wait on him anymore.

"He's not saying nothing," came Enid's voice.

The old lady had stepped out from behind her door, her arms folded across her chest. Her lilac sweatshirt hung baggy from her rounded shoulders.

"He's expecting me."

"I don't much like him," said Enid. "Something a bit off about him."

Georgie was alert to the risk of being overheard.

"I'm here to collect Cherry's photographs. He said I could have them."

"Oh darlin'," said the neighbour, suddenly appalled.

"What is it?"

"Well, that's what he's burning. Old pictures and that. He's taking them out of albums and putting them in this little fire pit thing. I thought it was a bit queer."

Enid had surely misunderstood. Georgie had inadvertently put the idea in her head. She was muddled.

"No," she said. "I'm taking the pictures home with me."

"I don't think you are, love."

"Enid. Are you sure? Are you absolutely sure?"

"He shouldn't be burning things anyway, in a built-up area. You're not allowed. All sorts of things this morning. Papers, pictures, clothes. It's terrible. Anti-social."

"That can't be right."

"Oh darlin'."

Georgie, in her confusion, backed into the bin and gripped onto it to steady herself. Looking down, a pale triangle caught her eye. It was fabric, poking out from under the lid and she recognised it at once. The Laura Ashley curtains, the pinks and blues vapid against the black plastic. She dropped her bag and flung the bin lid open. The curtains had been bundled up and dumped, and left-over food thrown on top of them. There was no question that Georgie was meant to see the corner and find them there. That's why the bin was out.

A sudden clanking sound made her turn back to the house. The letterbox had been opened and an item pushed through. She stepped forward and caught it. In her hand was the charred corner of a photograph. All she could make out were feet: her mother's slim angles in high-heels and her own five-year-old toes lined up along the edge of brown sandals.

"What have you done?" she whispered.

"Oh the cunt," said Enid. "The rotten old cunt."

They heard a voice from behind the door.

"Now leave me alone please. There's nothing left for you here, so you needn't come back."

"Why?" Georgie's voice was still feeble with disbelief.

Enid turned and left her, disappeared into her house. Georgie heard her words disappear with her: "I don't want no scene on my doorstep."

She stood with the curtains under her arm and the scorched corner of the photograph in her fist. As soon as her anger rose it collapsed into grief. She could shout at him again if she had the energy. She could threaten him. She could call the police, make a complaint right there where she stood. Instead, her cheeks and mouth already soaked with tears, she slumped by the door and called to him through the letterbox.

"Please," she begged him. "Please don't erase her. Don't burn anything more. I won't ask for anything, I won't take anything. Just don't destroy anything more."

As she left, she could just about hear the faint crackle of things burning, and took away with her the acrid smell of charred paper in her nostrils.

*

"Where were you?" she asked Beatrice that afternoon from her bed.

The girl looked forlorn as she took in the details of Georgie's visit to her mother's house. She had arrived in excitement at the bedroom door only to stop in her tracks at the sight of Georgie's desolate expression. Georgie had been crying so hard that she was shivering now, her arms and legs occasionally lifting in the echo of earlier convulsions.

"Are you having a panic attack?" asked Beatrice.

"Oh that's what it was," said Georgie, looking away from her, disgusted in herself and in Beatrice's bizarre insensitivity. But Georgie had come to realise that Beatrice took her lead from her in all things, including her manner and her preoccupations. If the girl was behaving in a singular and aberrant way, then it was because Georgie was emanating those exact characteristics.

"I'm nothing but hate now," she told Beatrice.

"Then so am I."

Georgie knew she was right. There was nothing left. Loathing propped up her frail body. Her mind was composed entirely of retribution. No room for anything else anywhere. If the girl was willing to come on this journey with her then so be it. She wasn't going to force her. She wasn't going to expend her energy caring.

"He's trying to remove her. His wiping out my mother."

"No," said Beatrice. "I don't think he is. I think he's trying to wipe *you* out. You're the one in the way. You're the one who won't let go and insists on reminding him."

Him and me, thought Georgie. Is that what this has all reduced itself to? Him or me.

27

In the car the following morning Beatrice said, entirely casually, innocently, like a child speculating about space flight: "I wonder what it feels like to kill someone. Not the guilt afterwards, not remorse or anything like that. But actually perpetrating the death of someone with your own hands. *With your own hands.* Knowing exactly what you're doing as you're doing it. What must that feel like?"

There was a silence, then, between them, not out of shock or the inability to follow up those spoken thoughts, but because they required further contemplation.

Georgie, who was driving, shuddered and looked for an excuse to stop the car. Said she was momentarily disorientated and pulled over to the kerb.

"Oh, I'm so sorry!" Beatrice exclaimed. "I shouldn't have said that."

"It's fine," Georgie soothed the younger woman as she yanked up the handbrake. "Absolutely fine."

But the truth was that she, too, had found herself considering the very same question the night before, unable to sleep, her stomach tightening as she tried to compose herself against another panic attack. All her thoughts had led to the same destination: that his existence was oppressive. What if he simply ceased to exist? Wouldn't that be the fairest outcome? The alternative was to see him coming and going from the red door, spending Cherry's plentiful money, enjoying his sudden good fortune, rewriting his history so that new acquaintances wouldn't even know how he came by his wealth, just assumed that he'd earned it. Thinking it through like this, seeing his grinning self-satisfaction in her mind, led her thoughts to simple, practical ones. How could she end him? How could she get away with it and, of course, what would be the cost to her? The mental cost, never mind the reputational one.

In the dark, the blind drawn down over the skylight, the house asleep beneath her, she asked herself what it would feel like – to end a human life. To hear the final breath, see the light go out and know that you had put it out. Would it be instantly transformative? Would it be awful? Would it be physically demanding? Would it be – for that moment – fascinating?

Would it be a relief?

With barely an hour or two of sleep, she had remained in bed that morning, the rain pattering on the skylight, while the others breakfasted without her. Sam came up and checked on her, asked her how her breathing was. She wanted to tell him that she was scared of her thoughts. But Sam wasn't staying, was growing increasingly gloomy about the onset of winter and the ordeal of getting a government through it, let alone himself. It was all too much for him, she thought, watching him go. Neither could reach out to the other and both knew it.

Benjamin…he had called up that he was leaving for work. That was all she got from him, a disjointed voice. And so, when Beatrice came upstairs, Georgie was ready, dressed and listless, insisting that they go out in the car for a while.

"Sure," said Beatrice. "But where?"

Just around, Georgie had said.

"We're not supposed to be making unnecessary journeys."

"It's necessary for my sanity," said Georgie, pulling on her cardigan and listening out for Sam's voice making phone calls.

Her sanity. Could there be a fainter, vaguer notion than her sanity right now? They drove along near-empty roads, turning corner after corner, as though the streets might hold the answers to their half-formed questions, and then suddenly Beatrice had broken the ice with her speculation and Georgie had been forced to pull over and wait for her breathing to calm itself. She didn't want Beatrice to notice how little control she had over her lungs, or indeed the steering wheel.

Georgie looked ahead through the rain-washed windscreen, not daring to glance at Beatrice, because Beatrice would simply take up the slack. Beatrice could divine exactly what Georgie was thinking and never questioned it, merely examined it and handed it back. *There*, she seemed to be saying, *you've thought it through. Now do something about it.* If Beatrice wasn't going to close down Georgie's thoughts, then she would simply have to carry on having them and – she knew – probably end up in a place she'd never been before. A place where most people would never go in their lives.

28

"You never wore slippers."

Georgie was talking to Cherry. She'd been doing it in a hazy half-sleep, the image of her mother sitting shivering on a park bench before her. Cherry was in tears, looking this way and that, hoping to make out her daughter so that she could be taken home. But someone got there first.

It was nearly midnight. Benjamin, on day shifts, was presumably asleep. Sam had come home tired and tense two hours before and gone to bed almost instantly. Georgie had wanted to tell him that maybe they should stick to their separate sleeping quarters a little while longer, that it would be for his own good. She knew she was unlikely to sleep and watched a film until she grew bored by it and switched off the light, dreading the dark hours ahead.

There was Cherry almost at once, alone on the bench, everyone else locked away, no one familiar that she could wave to or call over. And a space beside her that should have been filled with the one person who could calm and comfort her.

But it was wrong. That image of her mother jarred, and Georgie struggled to see it.

"You hated slippers," said Georgie, pulling herself up to sitting, reaching for the light. "And if you didn't know where you lived, how could he have taken you back there? Unless he'd followed you before. Followed *us*. Unless he...preyed on you."

The urge to be sick suddenly overwhelmed her and she doubled over and waited for the nausea to pass. Understanding, realising, relinquishing his version of events, didn't make things more palatable. They stirred in her such a desperate energy, that it was like an inner eruption. For a moment, she had to find her feet, return to her senses, but once she did, she knew she had to press on.

*

Her tread was so light that not a single floorboard on the loft stairs creaked. As she passed their old bedroom, she could hear Sam snoring through the closed door. Further down the landing was Benjamin's room. Her aim was to extricate Beatrice from Benjamin's arms and coax her downstairs where they could discuss things in the kitchen. It was barely past midnight. They couldn't have been asleep very long. Maybe Beatrice wasn't asleep at all.

Georgie waited beside Benjamin's closed door, tried to picture them. Young people slept entwined. She and Sam had done so in the early years. Now the very idea made her uncomfortable. Sharing a bed was bad enough. She wanted Beatrice but how could she disentangle the girl without waking her son? The risk seemed too great and yet she loitered by the door, as though Beatrice might sense her and emerge. Beatrice always came to her when she was needed, and she was so needed tonight.

Georgie left them, turned her back on the door and went in silence down the stairs, across the hall and into the kitchen.

*

Beatrice was there! Was she waiting for Georgie? It felt like it. She was at the table, looking out into the garden, seeing nothing surely, just letting her eyes rest on the blank of the night. Georgie spoke her name so as not to scare her, but the girl didn't so much as flinch when the light above the cooker went on.

"Do you often come down here in the night?" asked Georgie, settling opposite her.

"I don't sleep much," said Beatrice.

"I don't either." It felt like they were exchanging unremarkable life facts. Neither was moved or sympathetic.

Georgie got up to fill a glass with water and came back to her chair. Beatrice didn't speak in all that time, simply stared beyond the glass. The poor child, thought Georgie, she doesn't sleep because I don't.

"I'm sorry," she said, slowly rotating her glass on the tabletop.

"What for?"

"For complicating your life like this. For asking you to enter my messy thoughts."

The girl smiled and seemed, all at once, much older, much, much older. Georgie's age and with Georgie's experiences.

"Do you think I shouldn't be here? Do I make you uncomfortable?"

"No, you don't make me uncomfortable." Georgie sipped her water, searched for words. "You...you anticipate me. You know what I'm thinking. This morning, in the car, it was like you, I don't know, lifted the top of my head off and looked inside."

"I don't think," said the girl slowly, "that I need to lift the top of your head off. I think you make your feelings perfectly clear to me. I don't mean to intrude, though."

"No, I know you don't. And you don't intrude. Ever. You're just always there for me. What a sublimely useful characteristic. Hungry?"

Beatrice said she wasn't but appeared purposeless all the same. What had brought her to the kitchen, then? Was she there every night while they slept? Maybe it was a hang-over from when Benjamin did late shifts and she waited for him to come home. A damaged body clock.

Georgie wanted to ask the girl about the future. What was going to happen? She would know. She was still enough of an outsider to have an idea about how much everything would unravel. All the things Georgie wanted to say, all the loathing, could only be communicated to this girl. It was too unpalatable for everyone else.

"Eat something," said Beatrice. "Take care of yourself. Shore yourself up. I won't always be here."

Compliantly, Georgie looked around the kitchen for inspiration.

"You know I come and go. You know that."

"I do," said Georgie.

"And I'll go, soon."

And when you go, thought Georgie, all that will remain of you will be that broad smile, like the Chesire Cat's.

Georgie got up, suddenly hankering for the possibilities of the biscuit drawer. As her eyes swept the length of the kitchen and flashed past the French windows, she glimpsed a figure outside, disappearing into the shadowed depths of the back of the garden.

29

Beatrice was calling after her, wanting to know if she should call the police.

"No," said Georgie. She had opened the French windows at once, determined to catch him before he left the garden. Her heart was beating, and it was almost joyous, this adrenaline rush, the shaking awake that she needed. She felt ready, her teeth clenched, her fist balled. Where had it come from – this urgency to catch and hurt?

But Beatrice was beside herself. "Please be careful. How did he get in?"

The side passage. They always left it open for Benjamin when he came home from his night shift and he would close it after him. But he'd just changed shifts and nobody had thought of locking it again.

It was cold and Georgie was in her pyjamas, her feet bare. But the grass felt good on her soles, sharpening her will and her drive. How long had he been here? The sick bastard. Did he watch them? He was obsessed. Now the police would have a reason to charge him.

Beatrice was behind her. "Look," she said. "There's something on the bench."

Georgie strained to see anything more than a few feet away but, it was true, there was the lightest haze coming from the garden seat, from an item that was white. She felt she should go after him through the gate, catching him up before he reached the safe haven of Cherry's house, but she was drawn to the bench and whatever was on it. The two women made their way closer, Beatrice always a step or two behind.

"You mustn't be provoked, that's what he wants," she was saying. "I watched this thing on YouTube where they give you advice about dealing with narcissists, people who push your buttons and the thing is they want to get you all worked up. They want you do lose your rag and regret things afterwards. Don't – please don't rise to it."

Georgie was barely taking in the girl's babble. Oddly, she could visualise that YouTube film, seen plenty of similar things of late. Everything piling in, every face, every pointless memory. Why did Beatrice always insist on muddying her mind? She was by the bench now, the girl's words thinning into silence. There was a piece of paper on the seat, weighed down by a stone. Almost from the very moment she worked out that it was paper, she heard the first drops of the returning rain pattering on to it. She moved the stone and snatched it up.

"I'm going after him," she said.

"No," said Beatrice. "We're going back to the house. It's raining. Don't do anything stupid. Please. Don't rise to it."

Georgie hurried back, still that tick-tock, backwards-forwards of voices and faces in her head. Who to believe? What to do? In her hand was a piece of paper, carboard it felt like, stiff but damp.

She didn't want to see it but she had to at some point, even if it was a glimpse as it fell from her hand into the bin.

In the kitchen, the light was low and the corners haunted. They were quiet, arriving at the table as one, seemingly conjoined, breathing at the same pace. Neither had to say a word. Georgie dropped the paper on the tabletop and saw at once that it was a greetings card. *On Your Wedding Day*, it said on the front, in silver lettering, with a bouquet depicted in grey beneath it.

"What?" said Georgie.

"I didn't say anything," said Beatrice.

Georgie sat at the table and opened the card but was instantly startled and revulsed by the mass of scrawls and doodles inside, a mess, tangled verbiage, pencil marks scratched into the pristine white.

"You like untangling things," said a voice, perhaps Beatrice, perhaps not.

But not this, not this bizarre confusion, an eyesore, unnatural. Slowly, words lifted themselves up and out of the debris. *I love you, love you, love you.* And *my gorgeous boy.* And *you found me. Thank you.* Half-formed cursive, words running out mid-way, unscrolling themselves into grotesque pictures. *I have no one but you.* A face, ugly, drawn in a childish hand, its eyes black scribbles, long curly hair. *Hate her. Pig.*

Love you, love you, love you.

And under it.

Back, back, back.

Two people, two lovers, in a world of their own, waiting for their wedding to take place, to be called in by the registrar, getting carried away, playing, writing little love notes and hate notes. No one but each other. Fuck the rest of the world.

Beatrice must have been standing behind her, because when Georgie looked up she couldn't see her and she felt panic come slamming into hate.

"Don't be provoked," she heard.

Georgie was looking through the little house, all the way to the back garden, saw her mother's profile, the insensibility of it, the deadness. Imprint what you like on it, none of it means anything. But what if it did? What if her last conscious thoughts were that she'd been betrayed and abandoned? What if all that love that they had built over the years had been erased…and replaced by the sick subterfuge of this monster? And now he lived in comfort in the home that Cherry had created for herself, and his only entertainment was to stick a knife into the remaining daughter whenever it pleased him. This was hate. This was passionate, life-changing hate. Too precious a thing, too perfect to wait and let dissipate. Act, act now, so that you can savour it.

Georgie rushed to the hall, grabbed her raincoat and phone, stumbled into her shoes, and ran out into the sleeping silence of The Brake.

30

Don't stop to think or to reason. Don't remember, don't expect. Cradle the hate, keep it warm and functioning. Georgie, the worker-out, the layer-flat, the one who could see all the satisfying workings and the logic, was alive with a new beautiful purpose. The exquisite perfection of chaos. Unsolvable. Fall into it, thrash around in it. It's bigger than you, so let yourself be subsumed by it. Who knew what lay ahead? Certainly not her. Her shoulders, arms, fingers, tensing and releasing, needing to hold and to shake and damage. That was all that she was able to respond to.

Even the main road was empty, no cars rushing either way, nothing to impede her. She crossed it and on the other side, mounting the verge, her feet slipped on the wet grass. She fell forwards, her hands landing on the dark, glistening blades, the moisture seeping through her fingers. She lifted her hands to her face and marvelled at them, at the curled wet fingers, the half-formed fists.

Ahead the churchyard was a dark mass, more sensed than seen. She turned away from it, and toward the estate, over-sized street lamps, like floodlights, guiding her into its heart. Black windows, closed curtains, all the boxes shut and their human contents sealed in.

"I am not a daughter," she said aloud. The words were arriving and leaving, barely of her making. She laughed. "I'm not a daughter anymore."

Through the blocks she went, in and out of lamplight, as though she were emerging from tunnels each time. As she entered Cherry's square, she thought she heard the machine in her lungs, keeping her alive, and stopped suddenly. "You won't be yourself for a while," Naomi had said. "Let yourself be looked after." She saw the little tattoo, the word *love* on a pale, strong wrist. But it was Beatrice who appeared attached to the arm, smiling at her, *knowing* her. "Let me look after you. It's what I do best."

Did she really need them all? The people bringing her food, kissing her on her head, advising her, worrying for her, holding her back? Hadn't she always been alone, from the start? The thing that drove her – the hard, immutable thing – had never left her. The love from others had simply beguiled her but it wasn't like this, this predisposition for hate.

Across the square was the red door. Shut. But the curtains were open and there was a light on upstairs. She had no desire to look inside the house. She called up to him.

"Come out."

Georgie waited. Her voice had been firm and clear, but brief, the two words fired up and at him. No one would have woken on hearing them.

There! She saw him. His face had bobbed into view at the bedroom window. Just briefly, but long enough for her to see that he looked nervous. The thought that he might be enthralled her. Good.

She was bored with who she had tried to be. Her past was always there, the images lining up. Boring! This was her. The sorter-out, the methodical one. What method? There was no formula, just impulse. And endurance.

Revolting face. Deplorable, miserable mistake of a human. How did he think that he would measure up to Cherry's world? Or any decent, civilised place. He was a blood-sucker, a tick, hanging on.

"You preyed on her. On us," she said. She was in front of the door. She knew he was on the other side. "You heard the things we said, how we spoke to each other. You wanted that for yourself. You followed her home. You followed me home. That's how you work. You're vile. You're a sick fuck."

He was there. She heard him. In the silence of the estate, well past midnight, every sigh had its echo.

She put her head down to the letter box, opened it quickly, without warning. She saw him move away, flatten himself against the wall on the other side. The house smelled of bacon fat.

"Come out here now," she said.

"I'll call the police." He was scared. His voice was weaker even than normal.

"Go on then. I'll tell them how you entered my property."

She made out a whimper. "You can't prove I did any such thing."

She saw him scurry away from the front door.

"Come back. I'm not going away." Her voice was controlled and assertive. She was exhilarated by the sound of it. She closed the letter box, turned around and sat with her back against the door. She knew he was in the living room, listening. She didn't have to speak any louder. In the perfect stillness of the night, it would all reach him. There was nowhere for him to hide from her. "You're a parasite. You're a deadbeat. You preyed on her and you thought you could get away with it. You won't though. I won't let you. You're way out of your depth now. You won't do this to anyone else ever. I'll make sure of that."

He was there. There could be no doubt. She thought she heard an angry sob. He was moving closer.

"How on earth did you think you could move into someone's life, take it for your own, and no one would question it? You're just a common criminal. And a total imbecile."

He was back behind the door again. She was astonished at how acute her senses were, how aware she was of his scuttling presence.

For a moment there was nothing, just the night and the sleeping neighbours. Then he spoke and his voice was close, just a door's depth away.

"Do you know what I told her?"

Georgie refused to take up his line. She wouldn't let go of her own. "You're sick and disgusting. People are revolted by you."

"I told her the world was all closed up and gone away. That there was a nasty disease out there and everyone had fled for their lives and that we were the only two people left on the planet."

"You're like a child. Some fuckwitted child."

"It was just her and me and no one else. And, you know? She asked after you now and again and I said: *Oh Cheryl, she's gone and given up on you, like everyone else. Let's us live here together and look after each other.*"

"You're fucked up. A revolting little thug. You're the kind of person we laughed at. We laughed at people like you."

"And she said she loved me and she was eternally grateful to me. Because she'd been left all alone to fend for herself. She'd been betrayed by her own family."

"You're a disgusting liar. I can see through you."

"At night in bed…"

"Stop it!"

"I want you to picture us, together. In love. She was so loving. So young for her age...and very physical."

"Shut your fucking mouth."

Georgie was on her knees now, her face up at the letter box. She was holding it open and looking for him. Suddenly, his hand was in view.

"That's the ring she bought me. We chose it together online. The day it arrived was so happy. I'll never forget it. We were getting married."

Georgie shook the images from her mind. They were false. She wouldn't allow him to plant them there. One by one, she'd pull them up.

"She didn't buy you a ring. You used her money to buy it, that's all."

"We chose it together. She kissed my hand when she put it on. *Alan, you're everything to me.*"

"There's no ring. None of this is true. What do you take me for?"

Through the letterbox came the hand, pallid, spectral. The fingers flapped about to catch her attention.

"She put it on my finger the day we married."

A child's hand, waxy, bloodless. White, flaking knobs for knuckles. A cheap, ugly ring too large for the stick of a finger it clung on to.

Georgie grabbed the hand, held it tight, her nails digging into the skin. The Youngster cried out, tried to pull it away. She clenched her teeth, wrenched the hand back towards her, nearly toppling as she did so. The hand came to a thudding halt as his body hit the door on the other side. But still she pulled violently at it.

"I hate you, I hate you." She jerked the arm towards her, each time bringing the body crashing against the door. Whenever she pulled, a limp ragdoll collided with the wood. He didn't even cry out after the first time. She pulled at the arm, yanked it in towards her, thrilled with each juddering halt as he hit the door.

"I hate you. I hate you."

And then she let go and the arm slithered back through the letter box, and, on the other side of the door, a crumpling, collapsing sound. She tried to peer in but when she lifted the letter box, her fingers came into contact with something warm and soft. She touched it and brought some of it up to her eyes. Shorn skin, pulpy and glistening. She turned away from the house and stumbled to the pavement, waiting for the vomit and for the police.

PART TWO

1

It could have been two a.m. Or three. Or even six in the morning. She had no idea. They had taken her watch and phone away from her when she arrived and now she was in a room without a window and with such low, bluish lighting that the mind was instantly, apologetically confused.

Back in the cell, where she'd first been taken, they had suggested that she might want to sleep, rest her mind and be a little more refreshed when it came to the interview. She would need her wits about her and be able to answer questions clearly and accurately. She would have to be on the ball when it came to explaining herself. The inference was that the rest of her life might well depend on a few hours of sleep.

Rubbish. They weren't dealing with a child. She wouldn't sleep and told them that she wanted the interview to take place as soon as possible and that, yes, she'd talk to a lawyer first if that helped speed things up. And so they had taken her from the cell after a relatively short wait and led her along two starkly-lit corridors and brought her to the windowless room. They left her there with the simple instruction that she should sit at the table and that someone would be along shortly.

No, Georgie wouldn't sleep. Sleeping, thinking...those things were still under her control. She was only interested in the time, not because it mattered to her whether it was dark outside or dawn, but because she wanted to know how much of it she had lost. Without any means of measuring minutes, hours became undulating, imprecise things. She calculated only that she had glanced at least ten times at the back of her wrist and that it must have taken around ten minutes each time for her to have forgotten that she wasn't wearing her watch.

At work, she used to take it personally when her colleagues spent too long explaining an idea in a meeting, would feel her impatience stiffen her back and her face. It was *her* life they were eating into, her precious allotted remaining hours that could be much better spent elsewhere. And yet she could be slow, too, comically dilatory, dawdling over a word in a report, erasing it a dozen times as she thought of something else, then replacing it, then another word, then replacing that. Over and over. She would look up at the clock and an hour would have gone and she would only have a sentence to show for it. But what a thing of perfection. Because time was hers to use as she wished.

The floor in the interview room was hard – some advanced kind of very robust linoleum – but the walls, oddly, were soft. They looked like they were carpeted. Beige. It must have been for sound-proofing. Or shock-absorbing...or something that had been thought through anyway.

There was a table, pushed up against a wall, with four chairs, two opposing the other pair. She had chosen one against the wall so that she could occasionally lean her head against it and feel the rough carpet surface against her cheek. The air felt artificial, pumped in from somewhere, dusty. The smell coming off the tabletop was lemon disinfectant.

"This is just a moment," her mother told her years ago, comforting her after the departure of her first serious boyfriend. "In itself it's nothing. It's only when you stand back and look at it from a distance that you see it was part of something bigger. A chain of things. Better things. Or things that make more sense. It's just a moment. It will pass."

Why was there no clock in here? She was breathing used air, her hands on her lap so that she needn't touch the table, and she was concentrating on the bland, brown door, looking for the captivating, an error in the lamination perhaps, anything to stop her falling asleep.

Was it this morning or a million mornings ago that Beatrice had asked about how it felt to kill and the world had stopped and all those moments had suddenly collided, allowing her to see the chain that linked them? Such a precious, significant thing, to see that sequence of moments.

There was simply no way that she would succumb to sleep. If she slept then everything would be set back and any kind of resolution – and really any kind would do her – would be reached much further down the line. Keep awake, answer the questions, tell them a truth, go home.

*

The door opened. Georgie jerked her head up from her arms and tried to understand what was happening.

A woman was entering the room. She was around the same age as Georgie, squarely built, bulkier still in her navy-blue quilted coat. Thin white-blond hair rested on her collar as lightly as down.

But Georgie was looking beyond the woman, to the open door, disorientated by the sudden racket. Raised voices, cells locking and unlocking, someone complaining bitterly, someone even crying.

The woman shut the door carefully, pushing it quietly into place with both palms, then turned and looked around the room, her brain evidently busy, her eyes flitting about as she placed a large black tote bag on the table. Meanwhile, her hands scurried about inside the bag, exploring each corner. They surfaced several times, on each occasion with a prize: a printed-out form, a biro, a phone, a packet of gum, a spectacle case.

At last, she sat, directly opposite Georgie.

"No mask?" she asked.

"Asthma," said Georgie.

The visitor gave an unnecessary glance either side of her and then removed her own mask, to reveal a small, plump mouth and the scrubbed, reddened features of someone who had to wash in the early hours. "Then neither shall I. Our secret."

"You look tired," she added. "You should've taken up the offer of a good night's sleep. It's your statutory right."

Her voice was naturally low, with a little sprinkling of smoker's gravel. If anyone was tired, it was clearly her. She removed her coat and hung it on the chair back. "It's in your interest to be clear-headed, you know."

Georgie didn't wish to answer but watched her visitor remove her glasses from the case, clean them with her jumper and place them on her nose. Then she addressed herself to the form, raising the first page between two fingers like it was a soiled sheet.

"Georgina Helen Greenfield. Is that right?"

Georgie nodded.

"My name is Betsan Turner. And do just call me Betsan. I'm a solicitor. The duty sergeant will've told you that I was coming. Just to explain, we work on a rota basis. My turn to be called out this time."

"I'm sorry," said Georgie.

"What?" asked the solicitor, peering at her. "Oh, no, no. Not a problem. I expect to be called out. So…"

"What time is it, please?"

Betsan smiled and indicated that she should turn around. Georgie swivelled and saw at once the clock on the wall, directly behind her. How had she not noticed it?

"Two-twenty in the a.m. I bet you're shattered. Why didn't you make use of your right to a night's sleep?"

Why did Georgie need a clear head? What kind of ordeal was ahead that it demanded every iota of her mental strength? She could cope. She'd been doing this for years, shutting down parts of herself, while the outside gave every impression of a fully-functioning adult female. A very steady, efficient kind of one.

"You looked a bit out of it when I came in. Would you rather I come back later? I have other clients."

"I'm fine," Georgie replied. "There's absolutely no need. I was just thinking, that's all. I wasn't asleep."

"Oh yes?" said Betsan, merely by way of making conversation, her eyes off Georgie now and following the nib of her biro as it travelled down the side of the form. "Nothing too bleak, I hope."

"I was wondering what it must have been like to be one of the pharaoh's servants and be sealed alive into a tomb. It might have been soothing, in a way, to know that nothing else would happen to you ever again."

The solicitor's pen hovered.

"Right, OK. Well, that's a new one on me."

Georgie didn't really care if it was or wasn't. The solicitor had asked and she had answered her.

"Moving on," said Betsan, her eyes still on the sheet. "You know why you're here."

"Of course."

"You were arrested."

"I know."

"I'm here to give you impartial but expert advice," said Betsan. "I am totally independent of the police. Everything that happens in here is in complete confidence. Do you understand?"

Georgie nodded once again.

"We will go through the details of the arrest and decide on the best course of action. You're going to be questioned by two officers and they will decide whether to charge you and what to charge you with. It may be - and I won't jump the gun here - that the best thing will be for you to say nothing, particularly if you think you might be unwell. Depressed, that kind of thing. But it's a good idea if you're armed with some foreknowledge - about the kind of things they'll ask you. But as I've said, you may choose not to answer at all, in case you further incriminate yourself."

The solicitor stopped. There was the word, half-hidden but obvious. Criminal. Someone had to say it and to get the ball rolling.

*

"It's gone," Cherry had said. "And good riddance."

Yes, it was gone. The old garden, if you could even call it that, had been reduced to rubble and the rubble taken away in a skip. They had done it, a woman in her early forties, another pushing seventy, their hands encased in stiff leather gloves, taking turns to swing a sledgehammer. The old concrete flags were replaced by tasteful honey-brown stone pavers. A new garden.

As Georgie had stood there, admiring their work, she knew that both of them were thinking the same thing. Nothing stays the same. No one owns anything. One day those honey-brown slabs would go the way of the grey concrete.

*

"There's always death," said Betsan, looking up from the custody sheet with a playful set to her lips.

"I don't understand," said Georgie.

"The pharaoh thing. You said it must be soothing, nothing ever happening again. But the servants must surely have known they were going to die."

"That doesn't count. We all know that death will happen. It's hardly a surprise. I meant the unexpected. People springing things on you. Life springing things."

The solicitor's head tilted from side to side.

"It can't be nice though, incarceration for ever. Rotting away. When you've done nothing wrong but served your master faithfully."

"Oh, I don't know."

Betsan roused herself. "I won't lie. You're not my usual fare." Her eyes darted to the custody record in front of her, the biro once again moving up and down a typed column. "Let's see what you do for a living."

Georgie wanted her bed. The need was so intense and arrived so unexpectedly that there was a spasm in her throat and she struggled to swallow. What she realised she wanted was to watch the telly. The telly Sam had put there for her and she had disparaged.

Georgie looked down at her hands and noticed two things: that her fingers were tapping the tabletop manically, and that there was the faintest red-pink smudge on the joint of her right thumb. She moved her right hand down to her lap, away from sight.

"Nobody, but nobody, is comfortable in this situation," said Betsan. "Whether you're a serial offender or brought in, shell-shocked, with a first offence. One of the reasons I might suggest you don't answer questions later is if you're unwell."

"Unwell?"

"Liable to get upset and say all sorts of things. A bit emotional."

"Ah."

It was good, Georgie reflected, that they were the same age, same class, same profession. There was a confidence to both of them that meant they needn't worry about offending each other. They'd gone through enough to be able to do away with pleasantries or politeness.

"I'm fine mentally, though perhaps not a hundred percent physically," said Georgie. "If I don't get rest, I feel worse."

"Well, I did suggest that you get some sleep."

"Not here. How can anyone sleep here? I want to go home. I don't want to waste time."

The solicitor laid down the biro and arranged herself: her face, her hands, her position on her chair.

"How can I put this? We can't *assume* that you'll go home. It was a serious offence."

Georgie was amazed.

"He's alive, isn't he?"

"Ah," said Betsan. "It's intent, you see. It's what you intended to do that matters. And whether you intend to do it again."

"How can anyone know what my intention is?"

"They can't psychologically. But they can legally. They can't let someone go if there's a risk that she'll reoffend. And like I say, this is a serious offence. There was a weapon."

"There was no weapon," spluttered Georgie. "You don't know what you're talking about. A weapon!"

"I'm looking at the arrest details here."

Georgie turned away, calmed herself. Across the table was the lifeline. The adviser. She should listen. But she never cared to listen to anyone. She knew how things played out and she was always right. Or until he came into her life and broke the rules and the pattern and the peace. Could Betsan Turner be made to grasp that? And yet this dishevelled, tired functionary was just going through her professional paces, could have no inkling of all the ragged, torn-away moments that lay scattered in Georgie's memory.

Sam would be waking soon. He had to work on a government announcement about Christmas.

"You don't understand," Georgie told the solicitor.

"Make me understand. Talk me through what happened."

"This isn't the time or the place. Sorry."

Betsan couldn't help herself and laughed. She'd never heard that one. What an extraordinary individual. Naïve or obstinate? A little touched?

"This is *exactly* the time and place," she said. "Or maybe you don't understand precisely how much is at stake."

2

Georgie wasn't Betsan Turner's usual fare. But then Betsan, herself, wasn't a conventional kind of duty solicitor. She liked to talk and to discover. She should, perhaps, have been a social worker.

"Have you made your call?" she asked Georgie. "They told you that, right? That you can make a call. I strongly advise that you let someone know where you are."

Georgie hadn't but she didn't want to give her reasons. Beatrice would have sorted things out at home, told them what had happened, about the interloper in the back garden.

"Let's make sure all the details are correct. You're 52 years old. Your address is 14, The Brake, BR6 OHZ. What's that? Out Bromley way? Chislehurst?"

"Towards Orpington."

"Don't know that part of the world. Bit of a mystery to me."

That was always the attraction.

"Your family circumstances?"

"Married. With a son."

"They know where you are, right?"

She couldn't bear the thought of them. It was unfair – a kind of taunting – to even bring them up.

"I'm sorry you haven't slept," said Georgie. "Because of me."

"Oh if it wasn't you, it would be for someone else. I've got two others waiting in cells. A mad night. Usual stuff." Betsan delivered a puzzled smile. "But thank you for the sentiment."

Betsan returned to the safety of the custody record. As she bent over it, Georgie watched the lightest filaments of hair come sighing down around her ears and cheeks. When Betsan raised her head, she seemed taken aback to be stared at.

"Do you understand why you are here?"

"Yes."

"Because being clear on everything is very, very important. If you go into that police interview and say something…something ill-thought-out, the jury will eventually hear about it, don't worry about that. So, you're clear-headed?"

"I am."

"You said you weren't well."

"I wasn't. But then who *is* these days?"

"What? Oh, I see."

In hospital, they spoke to you like you were a precious child. Naomi had cared for her, had come back over and over again to check on her. And Beatrice, she was the same. *Can I get you anything?* had been her first words. *Are you comfortable? Have you got everything you need?*

"Occupation, occupation, occupation," muttered the solicitor under her breath. "You've said unemployed, is that right?"

"As good as," said Georgie.

"Ah, so you're not?"

"I've been on long-term sick leave and, well, I won't be working after this."

"You don't know that."

Georgie leant back on her chair and let a yawn emerge slowly and luxuriously. She glanced back to check the time. Half past two. By now she was used to the stale air and the disinfectant fumes. The pink-smeared hand was still under the table. The other slid across the table-top, left and right. The two women watched it.

"You haven't been charged yet," said Betsan. "Don't give up all hope."

Georgie didn't wear rings because she used to hate the sight of her plump fingers. Rings made them look like they were wearing tight belts around their fat stomachs. Sam joked that they weren't technically married if she didn't wear her wedding ring and that he might wander. But Sam would never wander. Sam loved their life, the quietness of it, the predictability. He whistled when he was at home, whatever he was up to. He once whistled when they were having sex.

"Hope?" she asked.

"Yes, it's a serious issue but at this point we can't be sure how they'll charge you. Or *if* they charge you."

"Oh come on."

"Well…"

"I'm not that green. Miss Turner, yesterday morning I woke up in my own bedroom, my husband was already getting ready for work downstairs. It was raining. I looked out of the window and a million things were going through my head but not this. So many things. Things with consequences. But not the thought that I wouldn't be waking up in the same place the following morning. I was brought in here, told my rights, had my coat and watch taken away, along with my cash, phone, and, briefly, my shoes. I was given this sweatshirt to put on over my pyjamas. I was scanned for sharp objects, was asked questions about my mental health, given a DNA swab and fingerprinted. Oh and breathalysed. Then I was put in a cell and I waited. Do you know what I couldn't quite cope with? Not knowing the time. I don't like not knowing the time. Otherwise, I understood perfectly what happened and why I was there and – most importantly – what it all meant. I am a criminal. Yesterday I wasn't. Today I am."

"No!" said the solicitor at once. "I don't think you should talk like that. You are the same person that woke up yesterday morning and looked out of your bedroom window. You've done something unthinking, that's all. Something stupid."

Georgie fixed the solicitor with a smile.

"I've never done anything unthinking in my life."

*

"Listen," said the solicitor with a little gee-up in her tone. "I know for someone like you this must be daunting. You've never been in trouble before, am I right? You're an upstanding member of society. You're a wife and a mother. A crime is a crime. Nothing changes that. But intention is everything. And that's what you need to tell me. Whether you actually intended to do this? Whether you took the weapon with you?"

"There was no weapon," sighed Georgie. Where had this idea come from?

"A lot of people are a little taken aback dealing with a lawyer. They don't come across us very much in their lives and they think we're going to smart-talk them or convince them to do something they're not really comfortable with. I want to assure you that, while I might be a paid professional, I am also an ordinary person underneath. I'm a mum, just like you. You mustn't feel intimidated. Yes, I have a law degree. But that doesn't mean I don't *get* you."

Georgie had no idea what they were talking about. How had they not even gone through the incident yet?

"Occupation," said Betsan, picking up her biro and clicking it a couple of times.

"I'm not currently employed."

"And when you were?"

"Is it necessary?"

Georgie had been bundled in a police car and driven in silence to the station, the radio crackling intermittently up front. She was paraded through the reception area, an officer taking down her details, calling her "my love" as though she needed calming and wrong-footing. She had been asked repeatedly if she understood what they were saying and all the while an angry young man, handcuffed, had been laughing – at her? At his own situation? – from a bench at the side. To have kept it inside, to have held back tears and forced herself not to say anything superfluous, had taken all her reserves of energy.

But now it was over. Now, like the faithful servant, she could be buried in the tomb and left to sleep for ever, to slip from sleep to death and forgetfulness. There was nothing left to worry about. Let it all play out. She could sleep.

"I'm a lawyer," she said.

"You're a *lawyer*?"

"Not like you. I've never practised criminal law. I'm in the Government Legal Service. I make statute. I am, I suppose, quite senior. And almost certainly now permanently excluded from the service."

"I never had you down as a lawyer."

Georgie was smiling.

"Oh darling, come on!" Cherry had laughed. "You're the least lawyerly person I know."

What would they call it? Grievous bodily harm? Wounding with intent? What kind of bloody lawyer was she if she had no idea what was ahead? Attempted murder. Was that it? Even when she looked deeply inside the words, buried herself in them, she couldn't quite see the workings or any way for her to come back up and out for air.

3

"You went to the house of Alan Shattock with the intention of confronting him about your mother's death. You say there was no knife."

"There *was* no knife. And I didn't wish to confront him about my mother's death."

Betsan looked so tired. What an appalling job she had, and most of it conducted in the middle of the night. Georgie wanted to be as helpful as possible.

"He came to my house, got in through the side door and left a piece of paper in the garden which he knew would upset me. He'd been goading me for weeks. Since before my mother died, in fact. I saw red, I'm afraid, and went round to see him. I didn't have a specific plan in mind. I wanted to tell him what I thought of him."

"He told the police that you attacked him with a knife."

"He's lying. He lies all the time. He lied to get himself into my mother's house and he continues to lie to keep me away from it."

"And the cuts on his arm?"

"The edges of the letterbox are very sharp. My mother used to joke about it. Called it a death trap. I pulled his arm through it and I don't deny that I hurt him as a result. And I don't deny that I'm glad."

"Yes, well we'll keep that view to ourselves, shall we?"

Georgie shrugged. All too late. Suddenly, she needed to ask Betsan pressing questions about how Sam's work was likely to react. About Benjamin's prospects. Would they have to move? How could Sam cope with leaving The Brake?

It had taken a while for them to get to the details of the incident. Betsan had seemed to need to skirt the issues first, build up a rapport. She had speculated on the "dryness" of Georgie's legal calling. "Not for me," she'd shuddered. "They were a funny lot, the ones who opted for constitutional law. Academic types mainly."

Georgie had said to herself: *Telly innards*.

Now that they were reaching the events of earlier that night, Georgie's mind was already racing ahead to the consequences. Who would look after her? This put-upon woman? Hardly.

"You called the police as soon as you realised what had happened. The severity of it."

"Did I? I don't remember."

"You did. I suspect you were in shock. Two officers arrived and found you sitting on the pavement. You said very little, only that you wanted them to check on the occupant of the house. They questioned the occupant and he told them that you had attacked him with a knife and that he'd escaped indoors in terror."

Georgie was in a daze of remembering.

"No. No it wasn't remotely like that. He never came outside. I pulled his arm through the letterbox."

"How on earth did you do that?"

"It's quite a large letterbox. He stuck his hand out to show me the wedding ring he claims my mother bought him."

Betsan seemed flummoxed.

"There's so much more to this, isn't there?"

"There's a lifetime," said Georgie.

"Well, I'd better hear it from the beginning. It will all be taken into account. But, just to nail this down, the police won't find a knife with his DNA on it?"

"They'll find a letterbox with his DNA on it, unless he's cleaned it."

Betsan was thinking aloud now.

"There are several degrees of assault charges in UK law. If you use a knife – which, as you say, you didn't – it can be anything from unlawful wounding to premeditated ABH. The decision to charge is based on a two-pronged test: whether it's in the public interest to do so and whether there will be a reasonable prospect of conviction. As far as I can tell, there is very little evidence in this situation, merely the complaint of the victim. However, he is undeniably injured. You're disputing the facts so maybe they won't charge you yet, not until they can get a medical report on his wounds."

"Can I go home in the meantime?"

"That's not for me to say. It might come down to a bail hearing. Come on, tell me everything that's relevant. How he came into your life. Don't forget there's a statutory defence of provocation. It's never too early to think of these things."

And so Georgie told her story. She'd recited the events so often in her mind that it came out easily and automatically. But it was strange how detached she was from it, as though she were reading the details of some other life. Nothing hurt her. There was nothing at all that outraged her. She watched the solicitor making her notes, followed the nib of the pen as it formed the words: *came between us, refused access, lied, manipulated.* She saw the ingenuity of it all at last, the way he had devised it and worked it. The details he had ascertained simply by listening to Georgie and Cherry or following them. Even that note that he'd left in her garden she now realised was a clumsy forgery. None of it had been written by Cherry, her tiny, elegant specific hand not visible on the page. But why? And why had she risen to it all? Why had she even given him the time of day?

Could that be it? That she *had* given him the time of day?

"Well," said Betsan, looking up from her notes. "What you're describing is a predatory marriage. It happens. All the elements are there."

A neat little case. Explicable. A wealthy ageing woman, losing her mind, is tricked into thinking that she's loved. But no, Cherry, even at her weakest, wouldn't fall for that. She didn't love this revolting specimen. She had no sexual interest in him. Was it pity, then?

"He ruined her life because she pitied him," said Georgie, in wonder.

"What?" asked the solicitor. "I don't think he ruined her life. I suspect he provided her with some companionship when no one else could. No, it's *your* life he's ruined. Or attempted to. All the damage has been inflicted on you. But listen, let's not talk about ruined reputations. People seem to think it's the end when they come here. But they shouldn't fear the law, they should embrace it and look to it for support. You make the law, Georgina. Didn't you ever wonder what it felt like to break one of your perfect edicts? Did you really think that everyone, everywhere can live up to those standards? No, not even you can.

"There's no real equality in life other than in the eyes of the law. Even the makers of it aren't exempt. You've found yourself in a world you never expected to visit. It's cold and unpleasant, with scary people and uniforms, but it's fair. And you shouldn't think yourself demeaned or diminished because you're suddenly part of it."

"I'm the same as every god-forsaken drug addict and recidivist, is that what you're saying?" said Georgie gloomily.

"Yes, yes you are. And so am I. All that's different are the circumstances. Who among us hasn't made a bad decision? But sometimes, when it's a really bad one, we have to pay the price of that decision before we can move on. It gives us the full stop we need."

You're just like everyone else, she was saying, and Georgie had never been cast so low in her life. All who laboured under the delusion of exceptionality did it via the comfort of money and education. That's how she had been brought up. The single child of a singular mother. Destined for better things. But it meant nothing, particularly under the queasy glare of the lighting in a police interview room.

"Now," said Betsan. "This will end up being a Crown Court case, the mitigations are so complicated. But I need to go to my next client. They're going to take you back to your cell and at some point very soon you're going to be interviewed. Let's go through what you'll say and see where it takes us. And I wish you every luck in this. Every strength."

An ordeal was ahead of her, that much she'd worked out. She'd have to step up to the mark. Her future, it seemed, depended on it. Actually no, her future was not of importance. Sam's and Benjamin's were in jeopardy and that's where bleakness truly lay, in the thought of what she might yet inflict on her loved ones, if she hadn't already done so. For her, it couldn't really get any worse. Her only pressing need now was to sleep. And she no longer cared where.

4

There were masked faces looking down at her.

She raised herself from the bench and tried to make out what was happening. The closest face was female. A young police officer, her large dark eyes kind and sympathetic.

"Mrs Greenfield, it's me, Leah. PC Hitchin. We've talked on the phone."

Georgie's sleep had been short but deep. No dreaming, no fitfulness. It was one of those rare sleeps that feel, on waking, that they've been a boundary between the troubled past and a new now.

"I need to take you to the interview room," said the policewoman. Her voice, now it was attached to a face, seemed warm and comfortable, not masculine at all. Exactly right.

Georgie scanned the cell, tried to place herself, reached a full grasp of the situation surprisingly quickly. "What time is it?" she asked.

"Nearly six."

She was led back down the corridor with the stark lighting, silent now, all the affronted shouting having evaporated with the night, and to another bland room, just like the one she'd been in with Betsan hours earlier. At some point Leah had slipped away and now Georgie was in the company of two plain-clothes officers.

"Will the solicitor be joining us?" she asked as she entered and sat at the table.

"No need," said one of the officers. They were as banal as the room, a man and a woman. Unremarkable people. Detectives, she assumed. Humourless. One sat opposite her, the other – the woman – a little away from the table and at the side. She had a laptop open and was tapping away as her colleague spoke.

"Georgina Helen Greenfield. You were brought here on the morning of Thursday October 29, 2020, that is today, after having been arrested on suspicion of assaulting Alan Julian Shattock of 7, Dene Close, Orpington, using a weapon."

The officer paused, licked his dry lips. Go on, thought Georgie. Get the spiel over with.

"You were told your rights and spoke to a duty solicitor."

Georgie nodded. Yes, yes, she knew all this. What a palaver. What dull officialdom. Did they think she would dispute any of it? Having licked and swallowed, the officer was setting off again.

"The complainant has since retracted the accusation and we have failed to find any evidence of a wound that might be caused by a weapon. In addition, there was no weapon at the scene or in your possession. We believe the accusation to have been entirely false. Now, normally Georgina, a retraction by the complainant is not enough for us to drop an assault charge but in this situation, it is very clear to us that there is absolutely no case we can lay before the Crown Prosecution Service. Therefore..."

"What do you mean, *entirely false?*" she interrupted the officer.

"At this stage, I cannot go into details as there may be a case pending against him."

"Wasting police time? You mean you think he lied to you?"

"I cannot go into the details."

There was a long pause while three sets of eyes skipped from one face to another. It was almost comical how novel this situation was, how quickly the police seemed on the backfoot. Georgie almost felt sorry for them.

"Thank you," she said quietly.

The male officer leant a little closer to her. "I've been a policeman for nearly twelve years and I've never come across this before. He was adamant. Said you had done nothing wrong, that he'd framed you."

Georgie had so many questions but even as they lined up, she knew they would not be answered. Not only had the Youngster retracted his accusation against her, but he had insisted on making his own guilt the primary focus. Why? Not to save her, surely. They detested each other. This was a competition. There had to be something in it for him. She had to feel something in return. Gratitude? Remorse?

She needed to get out now, tell Sam and Benjamin where she was and how things had ended. She craved the peace of The Brake, the privacy of it. She wanted to be sitting opposite Sam at the kitchen table, Radio 3 playing, Sam buried in his phone. She wanted to hear the door bang as Benjamin came home. She wanted to never leave her home again.

The chairs were pushed back and everyone stood up. There was almost a snort of disbelief in the male officer's voice as he showed her out and said that she was free to go.

5

Georgie was in such a trance that it took her a moment or two to realise that the officer behind the wheel was none other than PC Leah Hitchin.

As she had signed her release form and taken back her possessions, she was told that she could have a lift home. Everything was suddenly so fast and so confusing, the station lobby filling up once more with noisy customers, that she couldn't think straight.

She sat at the back and focused on the short dark hair of the officer in the front seat.

"What a night you've had," said Leah. "Did you manage to call your nearest and dearest?"

No, she hadn't. She was half hoping that she might slip back into the house unnoticed, go straight to bed and simply tell everyone later that she'd slept through breakfast. She couldn't recall what shift Benjamin was doing and Sam was so distant at the moment, bogged down in work, that the last thing she wanted was to complicate his life. Perhaps she could tell them that she got up early to watch the dawn. For the first time in her life.

"I won't drop you off outside your door, if you don't want me to. In case the neighbours talk."

Georgie nodded her appreciation. Not all police officers were humourless drones, then. She remembered Betsan, the duty solicitor, with sudden affection. There had been fellow-feeling there, which was remarkable given the situation. It was nothing to do with their legal background, everything to do with their age and sex. A silent sympathy. Anywhere she sensed an understanding, she clutched at it.

"I never found out anything about him," she said to Leah, shuffling a little further forward in her seat.

"That's because he's a nobody. You won't find anything on the internet about people who don't do anything."

"True, but no criminal record?"

"Nope. He's just one of those people who's kind of lived on the edge of everything. Not great at school, never had a career, no proper girlfriends, just drifted. Moved from one opportunity to the next. Not everyone has a plan."

"Will he be charged with wasting police time?"

Leah pulled a face via her rear-view mirror.

Georgie sat back in her seat and looked out of the window. The morning was emerging as not bright exactly, but softly yellow, a late-running autumn. The traffic was already shuffling. *Ha*, she thought. *I'm in a police car. I'm a senior government lawyer and I'm being driven back from having spent a night in a police cell facing assault charges.* Now it was over, she marvelled at how unmoved she was by any of it. She felt as though she was living each and every second, expecting nothing, knowing nothing. In a sense, she was looking out with new eyes.

Betsan hadn't made her ashamed to be a professional woman in such circumstances; she had almost allowed her to be proud to be human, to be part of the mess and misjudgement of ordinary life. There was adventure to be had, she suggested, even in weakness and deficiency. In our mistakes we join a new community, a motley one, true, but a forgiving fellowship. They were all walking amongst each other on the same plane. There was nowhere else to step, no way of avoiding each other.

"I'll tell you what, though," said Leah. "I'm interested in what he'll say. He won't give me any trouble. He wants to be picked up. I've come across people like that. They like to be handled. Weird."

"It's here," said Georgie. They were at the entrance to The Brake and she was of the same mind as Leah, it would be best not to have to explain to the neighbours why she was emerging from a patrol car.

Leah turned in the car, pulled up and kept the engine running.

"Will I be able to find out what happens to him?" asked Georgie, leaning down to the window.

"Of course. I'll call you."

The car left and Georgie stood on the verge. To her right, the morning traffic was building. To her left, the tranquility of The Brake called to her. But she was thinking of the policewoman's words. *He won't give me any trouble.* Leah was on her way to get him! That's why she had given Georgie the lift, because she was heading to the estate. In a few minutes, she would be knocking on the red door and the Youngster would emerge, ready and with his own version of a story that Georgie was fast forgetting. Why? What did he have to say for himself? She pictured a rumpled, pained, injured nobody. The peripheral kind of being that Leah had so often encountered but the rest of the busy, working world hadn't.

Georgie found that her feet were taking her away from The Brake and along the verge. She was waiting for a break in the traffic and she was crossing the main road. What was his intention? Was he trying to deflect attention from something else he had done? Maybe by telling the police that he had wrongly accused her, he was able to cover up something else. There had to be a hustle. There was surely a gameplan. She was running now. Her route to Cherry's house on foot would be at least as fast as Leah's roundabout approach in the car.

The estate was, as ever these days, a place of sounds, not sights. She heard children squabbling in an upstairs bedroom. Someone was emptying a bath and you could trace its gurgling rush through a downpipe. Her back was sore from sleeping on the cell bench, her legs stiff, her eyes prickling, but she couldn't rest. She wanted to see him for herself.

As she reached her mother's square, she noticed the police car parked in front of the house. Leah was talking on her phone as she scanned the upstairs windows. Enid was peering out from a crack in her door.

Leah turned as she saw Georgie approach.

"You're not supposed to be here."

"What's wrong?" asked Georgie.

"He's not coming out."

Georgie was scanning the house too, from top to bottom, looking for signs of movement, but the curtains were closed in each window. *It's your life he's ruined*, Betsan had said. *All the damage has been inflicted on you.* How might it all have turned out if Georgie had simply left them alone, had given her mother the benefit of the doubt? Had Georgie aided him in his game all along by falling for everything? She had been hot-headed and affronted and he had enjoyed the spectacle of her anger. Or maybe that was her hate talking. Maybe he had been as frightened of her as she had been repulsed by him. The battle was always theirs and no one else's.

"Enid! You've got to let me in."

The old woman was horrified. "I don't want a scene."

"You'll get a scene if you don't let me in. Just stand back. I'm going through to your garden."

Enid, alert to any potential wider disturbance, did as she was told and Georgie entered her house and, knowing the layout to the inch, made her way to the back door and let herself out. Enid's garden was made up of artificial grass and some pots of conifers, nothing else. Georgie could stand unhindered and inspect the back windows of next door and look for signs of life. Upstairs the bedroom curtains were closed. But downstairs the kitchen blinds were open and, Georgie knew, you could see a fair bit of the house through that window. The very window through which she'd seen the catatonic Cherry when she couldn't get to her.

She called to Enid to bring a chair. The old lady came swearing and hobbling out with a kitchen stool. As Georgie clambered over the fence she could hear, distantly, PC Hitchen's radio crackling. She landed in Georgie's courtyard and instantly saw the changes, the dead and drooping plants in their pots, the black charcoal ring where the fire pit had stood on the honey stone flags. Already the little bit of Eden was tarnished and ordinary, a bare shoot from the rose bush arching across the path, the hostas eaten into brown-edged lace, the soil beneath the fatsia crowded with weeds. How quickly the uncared-for became audacious, defiant in the face of its neglect. All nature – including human nature – came out fighting, was aggressive in its need for air and attention.

Georgie put her face up against the kitchen window, steeled herself against the sight of filth and disarray. Instead, her eyes landed at once on a heap on the kitchen floor, dark and humped, a strange stack of shoes and hair and leather. On the floor beside it, standing neatly and precisely in a row, three plastic pharmaceutical tubs for pills.

He was curled up, only the crown of his grey head visible beneath the canopy of the leather jacket. She watched and waited for the up and down, up and down, but there was none. Then she returned to the fence and calmly asked Enid to hand the chair over the top for her.

*

In the street, Georgie and Enid, as well as a couple of other neighbours, stood back and well out of the way as a group of three police officers used a battering ram to split and tear apart the bright red front door of Cherry's house.

6

Those meaningless moments, springing up one after the other in your path, then falling away behind you, they form a pattern. You can turn around and look at them and realise they're not meaningless at all. They have a beauty and a sense to them. But who ever thinks of looking back? Who has the time and mental means to untangle it all and see it for what it is? Most people would shy away from it, would prefer not to work it out and see where it's all leading. Most people would rather not know.

Georgie could never *not* know. Georgie always had to take it apart and to understand. And so here she was with it all lying around her, the past, the now, the precariousness of the future. Rubble.

The kitchen seemed cavernous, the garden beyond the window stark and dispiriting. None of it felt like home anymore. Furniture, appliances. Grass, a bench. Things. Things she couldn't enter and understand. She longed for the warmth of her son's skin as he bent to kiss her goodbye. She wanted to be in bed with Sam, the day over, reading their books, their shoulders together. For a second it occurred to her that they must all be out looking for her.

She had never made the phone call, had simply survived the night and come home.

She tried to look behind her, at the love of the past, from the people that mattered to her, but all she saw was him, the Youngster, in his leather jacket, far too stiff and overwhelming on his rickety frame. He had been so happy, in his defiant way. He wanted the world to see him.

She wasn't tired but she knew it was time to sleep. She got up and switched on the kettle, stood idly as it hissed into life.

The floorboards creaked above her and footsteps were coming downstairs. Benjamin arrived at the door.

"Tea, great. Can you add two extra mugs, please?"

Georgie's son was bleary with sleep. His hair was dishevelled. He was in his underpants and a T-shirt and his feet slapped across the tiles as he made his way to the fridge.

Georgie watched but didn't grasp. He wasn't asking her about her night, didn't comment on her absence and sudden appearance. Could it that he had no idea? How could 14, The Brake, have gone about its night in the same set formula, of undisturbed sleep and ignorance? Had Beatrice been so fainthearted and timorous that she hadn't even told Benjamin about Georgie going out into the rain in a coat and pyjamas to confront the Youngster? Or had Benjamin been so bored by his mother's antics by now that he'd brushed them aside?

"We're nearly out of milk. Shit." When Benjamin looked up from the fridge and at her, he appeared stunned. "Are you OK? You look...weird."

Georgie left the shuddering kettle and went and sat back down. "Where's your dad?"

"He left for work very early. Didn't want to disturb us. Some big announcement."

"And you? Where have you been?"

"Here. I've been here. We were asleep until about half an hour ago."

Upstairs a toilet flushed and Benjamin's door slammed.

"You didn't know?" Georgie's voice trailed off. She was on the verge of laughing except that she didn't have the energy for it. How on earth could she summon up the strength to tell them about everything that had happened? She'd hoped, at least, that they'd got half the picture. "Didn't Beatrice tell you? Doesn't she tell you anything, that girl?"

Benjamin's eyes were wide. "Beatrice?"

She felt piqued. Couldn't he see that she was on her last legs? But this wasn't the time to berate. She was losing them all so rapidly that she had to accept and succumb. She watched her son carry the milk carton to the work surface and share the last drops between the three mugs.

This was her son, was that right? The baby she'd held. No, he was just another person. A person she loved, but not hers anymore. She held out her arms to him but just as she raised them, the stairs creaked as someone came downstairs. A figure appeared at the kitchen door.

"Hey," said Benjamin, turning around with the kettle still in his hands. "Meet my mum."

"Hi," said a young woman. She was tall, at least as tall as Benjamin, with a long blond plait slung across one shoulder. She was in his dressing gown, her slim, tanned legs visible from under its hem.

"Not much milk, I'm afraid."

"No problem," smiled the stranger. She addressed Georgie confidently, as an equal. "Do you want me to go out and buy some?"

Georgie looked from one young person to the other.

"Oh, sorry," said Benjamin. "This is Laurie."

The girl waved and smiled again. She crossed the kitchen and huddled next to Benjamin, the pair of them giggling as they made the tea.

A mug was placed before Georgie but still she couldn't speak. She bit her lip and simply looked. They were in love. It was obvious. Benjamin was a baby before this woman, a grateful, excitable boy. And the young woman? Well, she was quietly euphoric.

"Let me run up and change and I'll go out and get more milk," Laurie suddenly exclaimed.

Mother and son watched the vision leave.

"I'll warm her tea up in the microwave when she gets back," Benjamin explained deliriously. He sat opposite his mother and drank from his mug before finally addressing the tense silence between them. "I know what you're thinking. You're thinking that I shouldn't have let her in, that she's not in our bubble. It's against the rules. But I squared it with Dad. He didn't like it at first. Didn't want her to come into contact with you or for you to know she was here – thought you'd find it an intrusion. But it's all right, Mum. It's all fine. I've kept her out of your way."

Georgie had listened but barely understood. "That's not what I'm thinking. You know it isn't."

Upstairs the shower door clanged shut.

"Don't look so worried. We're made to do tests at work every day. You're not in any harm."

"Benjamin!"

Both of them stiffened, both of them a little shocked by her vehemence. Georgie was deeply forlorn, dropped her head. Benjamin moved his chair closer to her.

"What have I done wrong, Mum?"

"Beatrice," she whispered, then gathered strength. "I loved her. I know you didn't, but she was good for me. She supported me. What did you do? Just kicked her out when this blond vision came along?"

Benjamin couldn't seem to comprehend. Was he that cold?

"Mum, Laurie and I have been seeing each other for months. We met at work. She graduated at the same time as me. Why are you talking about Beatrice?"

Georgie was sinking fast, grasping at words.

"Beatrice. She's your girlfriend."

He moved his chair even closer. Now they were inches apart and she was terrified to see how concerned he was about her.

"I had a girlfriend at school called Beatrice. I mean, that was years ago. I remember you liked her. I haven't seen her since then. Is that who you mean?"

She was trying to remember but when she attempted to picture this secondary school girlfriend, she was back with Naomi on the ward. She was listening to her talking about her sister. *Oh she's lovely, my gorgeous sis...she's the type you need beside you...she's the really good one...*

"Beatrice was here, with me. Every day. She's been watching over me ever since I came back from hospital. You saw her. You must have. You and your father. She was amongst us."

There was a tattoo of love. Whose was it? Naomi's? Beatrice's? There was caring and loving and listening. All the time in the world just for her.

We need people who smile a lot and make us feel good about things. They're like medicine.

Someone who understood, who could see the panic rising and calm her when she felt that tube in her throat and the terror of suffocation.

"Mum. Mum, it's OK. Just tell me what you think is going on here. Tell me your version."

"My version?"

And that was that. She was sunk. The last solid handhold had gone. Had it even been so solid? Benjamin was holding her.

"They told us at the hospital that it might take a long time for you to come right again. We shouldn't pull you up or question anything you say. Because who knows what happens when you come off a ventilator? Things might seem real to you."

Would it be wrong to release her tears in front of her child? Her head was on his shoulder. She had a feeling that the new girl must have come in because she felt Benjamin's collar bone jolt as he waved someone away.

"We're here for you, Dad and I. We always were. We've given you space and time, because we thought that's what you needed. Maybe your mind filled that space in its own comforting way."

"She was real."

"I know. But real is, well, it's kind of elastic, isn't it? Your real might not be my real."

"I'm sorry," she said through her tears.

Benjamin sat up and tried to catch her eye. What she saw looking back at her was pure benevolence. And that, of course, was exactly what Beatrice had been. A phantom of love. Or love made real. And the rest? Her. Her and her swarming dreams.

"I'm the one who's sorry," he said, with a sad smile. "I'm the one who let you down. Me and Dad, both of us, but mostly me, because Dad's had his own battles to fight. But it'll always be the three of us, I promise you."

She was nodding one second, shaking her head the next, taking it all in, failing to.

"I let you down badly, Mum. I could see you were suffering but I just didn't like to have anything to do with that nightmare of a man. He made my skin crawl. He was working his way into your life, just as he did with Grandma, and I couldn't stand the sight of him. Neither could Dad. We let you handle him all by yourself because we were embarrassed and ashamed. I feel terrible about that. I'll never forgive myself."

"The Youngster?" she asked, drying her face with the back of her hand.

He couldn't even bring himself to acknowledge the name that she and Cherry had given the interloper. Could it be, that they had hated him even more than she had? But both of them had run away from the problem, hoped it would go away. And now, of course, if had.

"Oh Benjamin," she said, and her heart was heavy with sadness and guilt. "I didn't tell you. I think the Youngster is dead."

7

Life was lived almost exclusively indoors. It was cold now and, apart from the supermarkets, there was nowhere to go. You saw joggers, more than you'd ever seen in your life, and families going for walks, but these were isolated moments, solitary people or sealed groups. Maybe it was different in London where nobody cared much for rules and the shops were so plentiful and their proprietors so canny that the regulations could be somehow got round. But out in the suburbs, where there were homes and little else, the air seemed voiceless and existence curbed and set aside.

In The Brake, Christmas lights were going up in front windows, but it seemed odd to Georgie that they should be there. What did they signify? Celebrations within? Who could possibly care? The Burge family had put a single string of anaemic fairy lights among the bare branches of their magnolia tree, which stood in the middle of the front lawn. Georgie looked out at it and felt sorry for the tree, having such meagre attention thrown at it. A mother and children from a family three doors down had put round a flyer calling on the neighbourhood to join them for a "doorstep carol service."

"I never want to hear the word doorstep again," said Sam, leaving the flyer on the hall stand.

Georgie and Sam didn't go for walks. They certainly didn't jog. At the weekend, they would get in the car and drive. For a couple of hours they could explore, trace the East Sussex boundary line from Tunbridge Wells to Rye. They never got out but would arrive home refreshed, like they'd had their allotted measure of exercise. And while they were on the road, they talked. They talked like they hadn't used their mouths before, relishing the picking apart of mundane events, burying in the process their fears and sorrows, their guilt and their regret. Bit by bit, Georgie told Sam about the events that led her to spending a brief night in a police cell. He never pushed, barely responded, waited for the details gifted to him. In return, he voiced all the doubts and worries he'd kept inside him for the past year. The mistakes he and his colleagues had made, the well-meant efforts, the panic and the anxiety. He was on the brink, he said, couldn't see a future for himself, ached for change. Georgie and Sam reminded themselves that they were no different to the rest of the world, wanting to do well, failing to be the superior beings that they once imagined they were. A mother and father. And husband and wife. Getting on a bit. Boring.

And if you saw them, this late middle-aged couple, getting out of the car on their return from another unremarkable outing, you'd see a tall, rather youthful husband, with greying, close-cut hair, and a serious frown of concentration, and a slim, rangy, simply-dressed wife, with a short, equally-greying bob, messy, some of it curls, some of it tangles. And you'd see the peaceful, well-negotiated love of two people who had, well…who had talked it through.

*

It was four days before Christmas, a Sunday, and Georgie had surprised Sam by saying that she wanted to go for a walk and was happy to go by herself. Sam had almost instantly understood.
"We're coming too," he said. "But we won't come inside."
Benjamin had already been for his daily walk with Laurie and declined. Any time the young couple could spend alone together in the house was clutched at and his parents understood and sympathised. And so, Georgie and Sam set off towards the main road and crossed it easily, as there was next to no traffic around.

*

The front door had gone through several stages, firstly a metal grill supplied by the police and then something cheap, pine and temporary, and now a black composite panel, with a small window and long brushed steel bar as a handle. It was an immensely ugly thing and yet seemed suitable and in keeping with the ever-changing facades of the neighbouring houses. The house itself was yellowing, could have done with a whitewash. There was a flashing "Noel" sign on the living room window sill.

The door was opened to her as soon as she arrived and she turned to look at her husband. Sam smiled reassuringly and said: "I'll wait for you."

*

She stood alone in the living room, her coat still on, while he clattered about in the kitchen. She saw at once that he'd wallpapered two of the walls – a design of what looked like huge white peonies with silvered edges. He'd done it well, if he himself had done it.

"Isn't it fine," he said. "I always wanted a feature wall. D'you like it?"

She said she did and accepted a mug of tea.

"And look at this!" He hurried to the small cupboard under the stairs and returned with a painting of a hunting scene. "From eBay. It's a real antique. It's the kind of thing you people like, right? Where shall I put it?"

He was awaiting her answer with some excitement and apprehension, it occurred to her.

"I like to put pictures on the stair wall," she said. "So you appreciate them going up."

The answer thrilled him.

"Yes, yes, that's what I was thinking, too. Great minds."

He went to the stairs and held the picture against the wall.

"Here? Or here?"

He was in profile and his adam's apple seemed huge, almost competing with his head. His hair was tied back in a ponytail and his black t-shirt was sprinkled with white flakes.

"I'll buy some more, shall I? Like a gallery. You could, maybe tell me what kind of thing is good."

The last time Georgie had seen the Youngster, it had been through a window and he'd been curled up and still. They had carried him out on a stretcher, but she had looked away, deeply uncomfortable and exhausted, and left for home with no wish to ever return. Now she was back, breaking the rules by entering another household. But he had asked her, and he'd done it through the police officer, Leah Hitchin, and so Georgie had taken it as a form of implicit permission. If anything, it was Sam's reputation to ruin, not hers, by being seen calling on other people's houses.

The Youngster had leant the picture against a step and was now indicating that she should sit down. She told him she was happy standing, given that she had to be elsewhere and didn't have much time.

"I wanted to show you that I've made the place nice. I thought you'd like that," he said.

What on earth did he want from her? To set her back? She couldn't afford to give any of herself to him. He'd almost certainly abuse it. And yet, it seemed like he, too, had moved on. And he appeared to want her approval of it.

"You must do what you like with it. It's yours," she said.

"Yes," he said, with satisfaction. "It is. It's mine."

She found herself sitting down, despite what she'd said about needing to go. She wasn't sure why she'd succumbed. He was on her mother's sofa while she was a few feet away on a new black leather armchair.

"What are your plans?" she asked him. She asked it without emotion, without any warmth or interest. It was something to say.

He was smiling as he thought about her question.

"To live my life," he said.

She kept nodding, couldn't stop. It covered her thoughts, her unanswerable questions.

"You've no intention of moving?" she asked eventually.

He seemed astonished.

"Why? Look at this? It's my house. I've always been happy here."

"Not always," she said.

"Ah," and he fell backwards into the sofa cushions, gleeful at a memory. "I don't count that. Anyway, it got you out of prison, didn't it? You were fool enough to call the police that night. I wouldn't have."

"I don't want to talk about that night," she said. "Not with you. Sorry."

He got up suddenly and she heard the fridge door opening and closing before he returned with a silver foil tray of salmon mousse hors d'oeuvres.

"Tesco seasonal fare," he announced, putting the tray on the coffee table.

"Did you love her?" she asked. "Did you even like her?"

The Youngster didn't so much as pause but packed his mouth with two of the mousse squares and kept an eye on the rest as he chewed.

She could wait. Not for ever, but for the time being. If she left with nothing, no enlightenment, then she was no worse off, after all. When he shoved the tray in her direction, she merely shook her head and kept her composure. Soon she could get up and go. She'd lost nothing.

The Youngster picked up another two of the hors d'oeuvres and dispatched them with the same zest as before. She wondered if he worked or claimed benefits. Did everything come from Cherry's savings? No, no, she wouldn't pursue it.

"Do you want to know about the end?" he asked.

She stood up suddenly.

"I.. I don't think so."

And sat straight back down again. She needed to leave and yet she was reaching for one of the mousses and putting it in her mouth. She looked everywhere but at him as she swallowed it.

The Youngster knocked on the table top with his knuckles and she was brought to attention.

"Please listen," he said. "I want you to. I've not been good to you. I've been the worst ever. I know that. You're clever and educated and professional. I shouldn't have dragged you down, but I wasn't myself. That night…I lied to the police just to get rid of you and then I regretted it. That's all."

"It's too late," she said. "You don't really think I want to hear this."

"Go then," he said and sat back, dropping his hands between his knees and resting his head on the back of the sofa, his adam's apple rising like a buoy.

She reached for another of the salmon mousses and, this time, held it in her palm. It was understood, then, that she wasn't going, that the moment was his and that there would be no further moments. He was looking up at the ceiling as he spoke.

"She didn't know anything. She didn't know who you were and she didn't know who I was. She was locked inside her own perfectly content little world. She loved to eat and to sit and look out at nothing. My job was just to keep her fed and looked after. Stop her accidentally getting hurt. Only I failed in the end. She fell. There in the kitchen. Nothing much, a little slip. Didn't hit her head or anything but just gave her inside a good shaking. I didn't even know it. She didn't know it. I took her to the hospital in case and she never came out. You think I was glad, don't you! You think I wanted it that way. You're wrong. My heart broke. I did love her. Not like that. We weren't really a couple. I'm not...I'm not the type to sleep with women, if you know what I mean."

"Why did you marry her?" Georgie's voice was tremulous.

"I don't know. To get back at you, I suppose. To make you think she loved me more than you. I was jealous. I told you, I'm not proud of how I behaved. But she didn't love me more than you. Nowhere near. She just needed me.

"She was beautiful and gorgeous and clever and I was so grateful to be with her. I wanted to treat her like a queen. Do you know what I mean? I wanted to serve her. I'd never felt like that before. I'd never had any purpose. You were right. I was a loser. If I died, no one would have noticed. *She* noticed me. She always spoke to me in the park. We laughed together. We had a…what's the word…a rapport.

"I loved how playful she was. Naughty. Up for fun. She loved life, right to the end."

Georgie listened and a single stream ran down her face.

"She talked to you, did you know that? Just babbling happily away. *Oh Georgie girl, stop tangling your hair like that.* Or, *come on darling, let's go shopping.* You were always there for her. It used to make me jealous, because I couldn't get through to her then. You were together and I had no look-in.

"But I loved being around her. I would have cared for her longer. Forever. I just wanted her to myself. I'm sorry."

The tears kept coming and when Georgie raised her hand to wipe her cheek, she smeared it with salmon mousse. In that moment of confusion, they looked at each other and nearly laughed.

Georgie was catching her breath, gulping, her voice struggling as she failed to suppress her tears.

"I can't forgive you," she said. "I'm sorry, I can't."

He turned his face to the side, his voice dulled, miserable. "I don't really blame you."

Now when the questions crowded, struggled for attention, she knew it was time to press them down and forget them. Questions never went away anyway. There would be more. Ones he couldn't answer. He'd said enough.

She was up again, desperate to end things here, and he turned back to look at her. He seemed inconsolable, his expression artless. It *was* a young face, after all. Not in years maybe, but in childish hopes. If she let him, he'd probably tell her about his time in care or in hostels, about a brutal childhood, about boredom and hopelessness. Probably even a fight over a pet rabbit. But she didn't want to know. Cherry had listened and opened a door to him. He had already probably long been ensconced by the time he waved at them nearly a year ago as they sat on the park bench. Her hopeful man-child, fondly known as the Youngster. Georgie hadn't been enough. Georgie was a grown woman with a life of her own. Cherry had a life, too, and it couldn't belong entirely to her daughter.

"The garden!" he said, trying to keep her there. "I don't know anything about gardens. I'd be grateful for any advice. She so loved that garden…but then you know that."

"I'm sorry," she said. "We're thinking about moving. Somewhere a bit more rural. You must work it out for yourself. It's not hard."

She had to leave him, there on Cherry's sofa, in Cherry's living room, with his glittery wallpaper and hunting scene, his salmon mousses, his astonishing pride, his passing contrition. His home. She had to leave his home.

But as she left, as she opened the new front door and looked for Sam further down the pavement, she felt confused and unsure of who she would see. A girl, perhaps? Always on the periphery, someone to come home to and recount what had happened. A vision of love and good sense, her conscience telling her to recover, to return, to improve. A face blurring the past with the present, an attachment, her core, her roots.

The clouds were low and hurrying across a grey-blue sky. She wouldn't look back, walked away. Behind her the door closed and her steps faltered. Sam was on the opposite corner. He held out his hand for her and indicated that they should leave. Somewhere, in another house, children were laughing, and in yet another, a girl called out for her mother.

Printed in Great Britain
by Amazon